Alan Sillitoe was born in 1928, and left school at fourteen to work in various factories until becoming an air traffic control assistant with the Ministry of Aircraft Production in 1945.

He enlisted in May 1946 into the RAFVR, and spent two years on active service in Malaya as a wireless operator. At the end of 1949 he was invalided out of the service with a hundred per cent disability pension.

He began writing, and lived for six years in France and Spain. His first stories were printed in the *Nottinghamshire Weekly Guardian*. In 1958 *Saturday Night and Sunday Morning* was published, and *The Loneliness of the Long Distance Runner*, which won the Hawthornden Prize for literature, came out the following year. Both these books were made into films.

Further works include *Key to the Door*, *The Ragman's Daughter* and *The General* (both also filmed), *The William Posters Trilogy*, *A Start in Life*, *Raw Material*, *The Widower's Son* – as well as six volumes of poetry. His latest books are *The Second Chance*, *Her Victory* and *The Lost Flying Boat*. With his wife, the poet Ruth Fainlight, he divides his time between London and a house in Kent.

By the same author

Fiction
*Saturday Night and
    Sunday Morning*
*The Loneliness of the Long-
    distance Runner*
The General
Key to the Door
The Ragman's Daughter
The Death of William Posters
A Tree on Fire
Guzman, Go Home
A Start in Life
Travels in Nihilon
Raw Material
Men, Women and Children
The Flame of Life
The Widower's Son
The Storyteller
The Second Chance
Her Victory
The Lost Flying Boat

Poetry
The Rats and Other Poems
*A Falling Out of Love
    and Other Poems*
*Love in the Environs
    of Voronezh*
Storm and Other Poems
*Snow on the North Side of
    Lucifer*
Sun Before Departure

Plays
*All Citizens Are Soldiers
    (with Ruth Fainlight)*
Three Plays

Non-fiction
Road to Volgograd

Essays
Mountains and Caverns

For children
*The City Adventures of
    Marmalade Jim*
Big John and the Stars
*The Incredible Fencing
    Fleas*
Marmalade Jim on the Farm
Marmalade Jim and the Fox

IMPRIMÉ EN FRANCE

ALAN SILLITOE

Down from the Hill

PANTHER
Granada Publishing

Panther Books
Granada Publishing Ltd
8 Grafton Street, London W1X 3LA

Published by Panther Books 1985

First published in Great Britain by
Granada Publishing 1984

Copyright © David Sillitoe 1984

ISBN 0-586-06377-3

Made and printed for
William Collins Sons & Co. Ltd, Glasgow

Set in Baskerville

CONTENTS

PART ONE

First Day

I

In those days, when you met a stranger on the road, the first question that could be put without giving offence, or that had any hope of getting a response, was to ask where he was from. If you found it difficult to remember his name, or unnecessary to know it because he or you would soon be gone, you referred to him by the name of the place he was born in, or had just walked or cycled from, such as Sheffield or Derby or Oswestry, as if he was the Lord Mayor of that town or, what would be more likely in most cases, the Lord Mayor's bastard.

The convenience of this system was that you could use it for either sex, because she also could have been the Lord Mayor's bastard. The only disadvantage was when two people came from the same place but that, strangely enough, hardly ever happened. In any case, you wouldn't use it except when the person had a name that was not easily remembered, or who didn't want to tell you his name, and even in a group there need only be one of them.

I had no intention of meeting anybody during my cycle tour, except Alice Sands. Most of the time I would be solo, because a mate who'd promised to come had let me down. I don't think Albert ever had any intention of coming, but he liked talking about the wonderful trip we would make, and if we hadn't steamed up the enthusiasm between us maybe I wouldn't have gone, either.

After our work in the factory, and sometimes during the day if things were slack, Albert liked to talk about it, because he had fallen out with his sweetheart, and needed something to take his mind off the misery. Because of this he seemed keener than I was, full of plans and routes and schemes and places to sleep, but a couple of days before we were due to start he kissed and made up with his girl, or said he had, and told me he could not possibly go. He was sorry.

So was I. Maybe I wouldn't go. But I did. I couldn't stop dead in my tracks, being geared to getting as far as I could from the factory under my own power during a week in summer. The idea of going off by myself into the unknown appealed to me. You never knew what might happen, though my hazy brain didn't conjure up anything special in the peaceful countryside of England. But you could always hope.

I knew that Albert had never intended coming, because he'd made no preparations. He'd saved no money, put no food aside, and hadn't even bought a repair outfit for his bike. When I told him I'd joined the Youth Hostels' as a way of sleeping cheap he didn't get busy and do the same. Even if he hadn't made it up with his girl he still wouldn't have come. And if he had he would have been such a burden I would soon have wished he hadn't.

That in a way was why I didn't want to meet anyone else on the trip, especially after getting used to the idea of being on my own. Perhaps it was all for the best. We'd done an eighty-mile spin to Skegness on the coast the year before, and Albert had toothache all across the flat part of Lincolnshire. There was a bitter headwind on the way out, and on the way back it rained for seventy miles. We slept the night in a cold pillbox on the beach, and I scrounged up and down for wood to keep a fire going, which made such smoke that we had sore eyes for six months. Next morning we cycled into Skegness town, if you can call it that, and all we ate at a café before starting back was a piece of toast with a few baked beans on top.

We took the hilly route over the wolds and through Wragby, and every place where we might have got something to eat was shuttered up because it was Sunday. It was also Easter. Lincoln was deserted. By dusk, some while after crossing the Trent near Dunham, we were nearly dropping dead with cold and hunger. It was absolutely true, I told a mate at work. I never thought it would happen in a civilized country, even though there was a war on. We even had some money in our pockets, or at least I did. And if it was like that with us, how would it have been for a prisoner of war on the run? A man in Lincoln jail, we decided – though the laughs didn't last very long – would have had less chance of making a clean break than if he'd been in Dartmoor. He'd have starved to death before he got five miles.

We called at a couple of houses in a village to see whether anybody would put us up for the night, but at both they shut the door in our faces as if we were beggars, not realizing what an SOS situation it was. They couldn't even tell us where we might find a bed. We had money. It made no difference.

In Tuxford, after seventy miles from the pillbox, now remembered as the cosiest nook we'd ever known, I spent my last seven bob on bed and breakfast for us both. The woman fed us sardines on toast, then put us into one big bed where we slept like the dead.

Albert had bellyached all the way, and the next morning he could only think of getting straight home, like a pigeon back to its coop. I was for doing a few zigzags through Sherwood Forest, so we parted, and I felt ten tons lighter.

This time I was glad to be on my own. For one thing I didn't have to drag anybody out of bed and get them moving. Albert was in the Cadets like me, and I had woken him often for Sunday morning parade. I would go into his house at eight o'clock without knocking, when everybody was asleep, then make my way up to the attic room and pull him out of bed from among his four brothers. His old man had been too blindoe on getting home the night before even to lock the door, and when I once said, 'Aren't you frightened of somebody coming in, Mr Colston, and taking something?' he laughed and answered: 'What, like one of me kids?'

I packed my saddlebag in the backyard with a spare shirt, a towel, a pair of socks, needle-and-thread, an anti-gas cape to keep off the rain which had been issued in the Cadets, as well as a three-piece razor, brush and shaving soap. If I went without a shave I looked as if I needed a wash, though I only did it twice a week. My father said I shouldn't shave before I had to, but I'd heard that when you joined up you had to shave whether you needed to or not, so I thought I might as well get used to it. I also carried a three-mile-to-an-inch National Road Atlas, and a guide book, and in my saddlebag I'd hidden a half-crown packet of French letters in case I needed them with Alice Sands or whoever else I might click with. You never knew. I'd used plenty in the last couple of years, not wanting to get anyone into trouble, especially myself.

The bag wasn't even full as I rattled down the cobblestoned street on my reconditioned three-speed machine bought the year before for ten quid. It was no boneshaker, though not new either, because no bikes had been made during the war except for the army. My

12

mother had bought it me, saying she'd got the money from Uncle Fred, her brother, though how she could have done when he was in a Home and was so far gone that he didn't know whether he was coming or going was more than I could understand. But she said he wasn't so daft that he couldn't make me a present, and I was glad enough to believe her.

With nearly three pounds cash in my pocket I was made. The girl I was going out with in a half-hearted way wouldn't be seen dead on a bike, and didn't care if I went off on my own. I wasn't sorry to leave her for a week, and she shed no tears at seeing me go, because there were some things you couldn't share. She was a strait-laced ugly little thing with buck teeth, and I didn't think she'd ever liked me. She lived on a private housing estate, and her parents who worked in the corporation offices had taken her on a fortnight's holiday to Llandudno. I'd met her at a Cadet dance one Saturday night, and because I was a sergeant she thought there was more to me than there was. I'd told myself often, and knew it for a fact. When Albert saw her he said he thought she was the sort that would fuck like a rabbit in a thunderstorm, but I said I didn't think she did, but that if she did she didn't with me. But he didn't believe me, because otherwise how was it I kept going out with her? I thought it was no use telling him that if someone fascinated me, no matter how little, I found it hard to stop seeing them – though I had come to the end of my tether with Janice.

II

Chestnut trees hung over the long brick wall of Wollaton Park as if offering the gift of a spiked conker to everybody who passed. They were light green and

13

looked good enough to eat, so it was obvious they were poison. One had blown off and rolled into the road, or been kicked there. The front tyre shot it back, and though the wheel wobbled I didn't come off. Regaining a straight line, I worked out how many revolutions of the wheel were needed to get me a hundred yards forward.

Otherwise my mind stayed blank, letting me enjoy the breeze and the road that was still flat. Not long ago the leaves would have been ruined by smoke-screens set going every night during air raids so that German bombers wouldn't know where they were, but now near the end of July and the war in Europe over they were still rich enough to smell good in the breeze.

I was on my own but didn't feel dull as I turned onto the main road for Derby, still on page 150 of my atlas. I wanted to go onto as many different pages as I could, and the only way was to make as big a circuit as possible from Nottingham.

Sleeved by manor walls on one side, and university buildings on the other, I coasted west by the happy scrumping grounds of Bramcote Hills. A base of cloud hung round their tops which, not knowing whether it was damp or dry, made it impossible to predict what sort of a day it would be. Pale edges above blended with the sky, and the odd scrap of following wind helped me along. Whose side God was on I couldn't say, so didn't feel threatened.

I pedalled rapidly for a while. Being mobile, I was without a care in the world. If I was on piece-work in the factory, being paid so much for a hundred revolutions of the wheels, I would have made a fortune. But I was better out here than in the factory. There was no comparison. For most of the morning I'd stand at

14

my machine going mad—headed to get as many done as I could, my energy powered by the idea that this was definitely not the life for me. It had been all right when I was fourteen because I didn't know enough to want something different, but now I was getting fed-up, though nobody around me would have thought so, because dissatisfaction only made me go faster and seem dead keen.

An old man, whose walking stick I noticed before looking up at him, wore a collar and tie, and stared at me with thoughts of his own, and I didn't want to connect with him, or get into the darkness behind his fixed eyes, but sped along so that he was out of my way in a second. But I took a Technicolor photo-snapshot which stayed in my mind for good. He wanted to be me, I thought, and I supposed it was understandable on such a morning. I didn't care whether I was me or not, because it didn't matter. Being me, I had no need to worry. That's what he wanted to be like, and who could blame him? Which set me to wondering if I would come across anybody on the trip who I would more like to be than I was myself.

Such a feeling didn't last and, with nothing further on my mind, I went on, already smelling the soil of fields instead of the bike oil which I had laced on sprockets and hubs the night before. The funnel of my route was pleasant, and did not make me tired, though soot from Stanton Iron Works was also in my nostrils. The Russians had captured Berlin three months ago but the firm still worked, making stuff for peace now, smoke from chimneys trying to nibble the sky but vanishing in it.

For a while before Stapleford the road was clear, a novelty I liked. I had it to myself till a blind man with no collar and tie but highly polished boots crossed between two cottages. He waved on hearing the tick of my wheels. I signalled back, as if I was the Prince of Wales. An overtaking army lorry nearly bumped my handlebars, and I shook my fist at the laced-up canvas.

On the way to Skegness last year me and Albert saw a lorry overturned by the roadside near Radcliffe. The driver lay outside his cab with a jagged rip down his forehead as if painted with a piece of red crayon. I supposed nobody had passed that way for ages, so we went to the village and told the policeman, who got on his bike and came back with us. It was the first dead body I'd seen, and it didn't seem real, a bit of rammel thrown onto the rubbish tips. I felt tired for a couple of hours afterwards, which might have been because we were pedalling into the wind. We went back to the accident, wanting another look at the corpse, and to see whether an ambulance would come to cart him off.

The body had gone, though the lorry was still capsized on the verge, and there were bloodstains on the grass. The bobby laughed at our surprise. 'There are more things in heaven and earth than are dreamt of in your philosophy.'

'Who said that?' I knew it wasn't him.

He got back on his bike. 'Shakespeare'.

I might have known it. 'The dead man was tall, thin-faced, and had dark hair,' I said. 'He wore a boiler suit as well, and looked about thirty. I expect he's got a long scar down his forehead by now.'

'Maybe I'll catch the rogue up.' The copper looked very hard-faced. 'He can't get far if he's as dead as you said he was.' Then he gave a knowing laugh to show how daft he thought we were, and went towards Nottingham, while me and Albert steamed on to Grantham. But we didn't see the man we thought had been dead. Maybe he'd crawled into a field and kicked

16

the bucket, and if so I wondered whether he would ever be found, though the police had got the stolen lorry back and all that was on it. The driver must have gone to sleep at the wheel, or been a bit too quick in his getaway.

Stapleford seemed to go on forever. The road was narrow, with houses on either side, but the way went downhill, and as the town came to an end I pedalled the Erewash bridge, beyond which the buildings became Sandiacre for another three miles.

A card in a shop window saying FILLED COBS made me feel hungry, though I wasn't. I wondered when I would reach country, but it was only ten o'clock so I didn't care. When it was a bit uphill into Derbyshire my three-speed slipped, as if the bike wanted to turn round and take me back. I wasn't superstitious, and leaned the frame against a wasteground fence, to fiddle the screw along the wire till the grip was firm again.

Sandiacre seemed to drag on forever. I wanted to close my eyes and open them when I got to green fields, but I could no more do that than ride with no hands – unless a special sort of wireless was invented that would play music in my ears when a car or the kerb was coming close. Until then all I could do was push on, podged as I still felt from a plate of dried egg for breakfast.

I was fit and full of energy, and in any case it was only fifty miles to Stafford where I had made plans to see Alice Sands again. As for where I was finally heading I didn't know, but first I was going to see her. Whenever she came into my mind I smelt the roses in the gardens of Wishdale Abbey, where we had walked one evening after meeting on a lane near the aerodrome.

17

Albert was with me, so we'd made a foursome with Alice and her girlfriend Gwen.

I lagged behind with Alice, and we kissed among the tall rose bushes growing wild all over the place. The Abbey was in ruins because it had caught fire when soldiers had been billeted there. I had never smelt anything so sweet out of nature as those roses. They were nearly as sweet as peardrops, and the garden was a jungle, saturated with weeks of spring rain. Among the smell of sweetness the rain had also washed down a tang of burnt rafters from inside the blackened walls. We were cut off from the world, and when I kissed Alice she didn't say anything to stop me.

My hand was on her ginger hair, and I felt her small teeth through the kisses. I tried to undo the top button of her blouse, as if only playfully, but she pushed my hand away. She neither called out nor made a fuss, so I didn't try again, though later I wondered whether I ought to have done. I couldn't tell whether she wanted me to or not.

Wet drops from the highest roses had fallen on her hair, and she shook them away. Albert and Gwen weren't getting on very well, and shouted for me and Alice to come out because it was getting late, and though Alice was enjoying herself (but without saying much) she used their panmouthing as an excuse and said hadn't we better go? I got a few more kisses, and pressed her so close I never wanted to free myself. When I walked back into camp everyone laughed at the lipstick on my Cadet uniform.

I asked her for her address, and wrote to her. More than I expected, a letter came straight back, not exactly a love letter, but she wrote four pages, and said she wanted to see me again, and when would I come to Stafford? Her father, she told me, was a farmer, and she

18

lived at home, helping the family. She was quiet and serious, not like the girls I'd been used to from Nottingham, where for some reason I hadn't been able to meet anyone like her.

I thought of her all the time I worked at my machine, wanting only to go back to Stafford. But working in a factory I couldn't get time off, and the weekends never seemed long enough. I talked about it to Albert, who said that even though he was courting his girl in Nottingham, he wouldn't mind going to Stafford either, to see what he could do about that little bit of unfinished business with Gwen. In the end he copped out, and I was going there on my own.

What I remembered most about Alice was her mouth, because its shape was something I hadn't been close to before. It was meant for coming towards mine, that was all I knew when I was with her. She had doll's lips, but they were living, reminding me of a film star's whose name I couldn't remember. She had clear hazel eyes, and a fringe of auburn hair in a line across her forehead, and pale skin with a few freckles. Albert said he didn't think much of her, but I saw there was more to her than he could ever know, though what it was I couldn't analyse or give a name to.

I wasn't able to stop looking at her face while walking among the rose bushes of Wishdale Abbey, and could only risk one-second glances because when she once caught me she got angry and asked what was I staring at? She had an old-fashioned look, as they say, as if she knew very well what went on behind her smile and at the back of her eyes, but she wasn't telling me or anybody else, never on your life.

But her lips also showed that she felt there was something about the look that she didn't know, and would very much like to know, though there wasn't much hope of her being able to do so. Her smile gave her an expression which made her more real to me, because she seemed as unsure of everything as I was. I also thought it would be easy for us to get on together, though I couldn't be certain she would ever give me a proper chance.

Perhaps because she thought she knew more than what she didn't know, she kept herself to herself. On the other hand, she sometimes looked at me as if she might want to tell me what she knew, but didn't know how to do it. She was looking for someone who would make it easy for her to give it to. I hadn't thought so much about a girl or anybody else before.

Albert said he didn't know what I was talking about. Neither did I. He said I was going off my head. I thought there might be some truth in this, but couldn't admit it to somebody like him. 'You've got to stop thinking about her,' he said. 'You've got it bad, and that ain't good.'

He was trying to shame me, but as the weeks went by I had it less and less bad, though now that I had set out to meet Alice Sands again all my feelings about her were coming back, and I was getting it just as bad as I had before. It occurred to me as I rode along that Albert had also copped out because he thought I was too serious about her, and that no matter how well he got on with Gwen – and the signs hadn't been all that good – he would be left out. The last thing you could do was get serious. To somebody like Albert it was treachery, even though he was serious with a girl of his own.

Alice and Gwen expected both of us to come to Stafford, and I hadn't written to say there would only be me, in case they used it as a reason to call the date off. Alice had sent her phone number so that I could tell

20

them, she said, when we reached Stafford. I hadn't known anyone with a telephone before, I realized, passing the Blue Ball pub at Risley, which landmark put me well onto page 149 of the atlas.

After Risley the real country began. For at least a mile there were no houses by the roadside. There was space beyond the hedges, which was what I had come out for. I even forgot Alice, until the first buildings of Borrowash, when Derby town seemed already breathing in my face. Then she came back so intensely I couldn't believe I'd be seeing her that afternoon. The second time was never as good as the first, I thought, though if you got through it, the rest might not be so bad. Then again you could be trapped into a bout of courting which might last for life, and that would be worse.

Though I had gone out more than once with girls since I was fourteen I wouldn't hurry too much towards Stafford in case Alice decided not to be interested, which was possible, seeing I was turning up without Albert to occupy Gwen. On the other hand, things might go better than I could dream of, but I still saw the difficulties in courting a girl who lived fifty miles away. To ride there and back after work in the evening wasn't feasible. Even at weekends it would be a bit of a push, though not out of the question, except that a couple of nights bed-and-breakfast, if I could find a place, would put me back a bob or two. I preferred not to think about such details, unless to wonder whether her father wouldn't let me sleep in one of his barns and thus save my spending money, because I realized, for no good reason at all, that the more vivid she had been on first meeting, and the more I felt myself in love with her, the less did I want to see her again. I didn't know what I wanted to do, and that was a fact, yet I pedalled on, and couldn't have turned back even if there had been fire in front and a cool featherbed behind.

III

Stopping to buy a packet of twenty Player's, I was in a sweat because the shopkeeper had to serve a gang of kids with bottles of Tizer and a week's supply of comics before getting to me. There was a smell of magazines and aniseed balls, sherbet and ink, and I looked through the row of knitting patterns to make sure my bike didn't vanish from the kerb.

I was impatient and, stuffing the fags away, Spitfired along the straight canyon of factories and small houses that led to the middle of Derby. Tattered election posters were on the walls, blue and red and yellow, some half-covered with Food Office adverts.

I fancied a cup of tea at a stall in the market place, but drank my bottle of water, and pushed on till I could stop and smoke a cigarette while looking in the window of Butler's bookshop. There was a display of drawing instruments and foreign dictionaries, and books about the war, and politics, and I thought that if I could afford it I would buy some of them.

Back on the road I asked a bloke if I was going the right way for Uttoxeter. My atlas wasn't good enough for getting me through towns because, in order to comply with the Control of Maps Order, street plans had been cut out of this edition. I'd read in a book somewhere that Uttoxeter should be pronounced *Uxyter*, but it seemed a bit daft to use such a word, and in any case the man understood me, and pointed the way.

I got on my saddle, wanting to be shut of Derby and start biking through unknown territory – *terra incognita* –

where I expected to feel as if I was on an exploring trip. Towards Mickleover it was a bit hilly, but I was surrounded by real country again. I was puffed, though, and pushed the last bit up the gradient, though more because I felt bored than that my lungs were ready to burst, which reminded me (and I wish it hadn't) that a week ago I had been with Albert to have an X-ray at the General Hospital, to see whether or not we had got TB.

The gaffer at the factory said that all who worked for him should go, and though Albert and me didn't want to bother we went in case the others thought we were afraid. We coughed all the way for a lark, and laughed at the prospect of dying if it turned out we'd got the disease, but the next night at the youth club we heard that a girl's sister who'd had an X-ray two weeks before had received a letter saying she had it, and was to go to bed straightaway till they found a place for her in Newstead sanatorium. We'd always known she was as thin as a rake, but had never connected it with her coffin-cough.

We stopped laughing then and began to think it might already have got a grip on us as well, though there was still a fortnight to go before we would get a letter telling us for certain. It was like waiting to find out whether you'd been sentenced to death or not. It occurred to me now that maybe Albert had backed out of the trip because of that. He wanted to be at home if the letter came while we were away. But I couldn't believe it. He was as healthy as a bullock.

I didn't think I had consumption, or that I was dying, because I'd never felt better in my life. But before having the X-ray taken I'd not known whether I felt good or not, so that I began to wonder and stay awake at night hoping to God I hadn't got it, because all the people I knew who had had it had died of it. If you have it, you know you'll die from it. And if you die of it, you'll know you'd had it, except by then you know nothing at all. So before you know you've got it, but while thinking you might have it, you wonder what you can do so as not to get it, but end up thinking there's nothing at all to be done, because if you've got it you've got it and if you haven't you haven't, though you want to know one way or the other before the worry kills you.

If the worry does kill you, it doesn't matter whether you've got it or not, because you're dead anyway. So if the worry is going to kill you, you can stop worrying about whether or not you've got TB. If you stop worrying, the worry will no longer kill you, but you still might have it, and if you do you'll have to start worrying all over again. But if I do have it, I thought, I still don't want to know, either, because if I haven't got it, I can still get it, and more than anything else I want nothing to do with it, and wish I had never been forced by the gaffer to go for an X-ray.

When I didn't think about it I was all right. When I did chew it over, I got into a mood which even fresh air and green country couldn't blow away, not while the mood seemed to weigh more than my own body. But the biggest killer, and I knew it for sure, was that if I had got TB Alice wouldn't want to know me, no matter how near or far away I lived, and nobody would blame her, me least of all, because no other girl would want to know me either. If I had to have an illness I'd rather have the one Uncle Fred had got, and that's bad enough, his being off his head most of the time, but more than anything I'd rather have nothing, and in the moments when I didn't worry that's what I hoped I had.

A youth standing by the church at Etwall asked

whether he was on the right road for Uttoxeter. I could tell he wasn't local, otherwise he would have said *Uxyter*, and if he had been born in the district he wouldn't have asked the way there. He seemed a bit older than me. His sleek racing bike with back bag and panniers, toe-clips, rolled-up cape, waterbottle and pump, leaned nearby. He was dressed in khaki shorts that came to his knees, and wore a jersey instead of a coat, looking very spruce with fair hair and white hands.

'I've been looking at the church.'

It seemed a funny habit to get into. He could have been round the back for a piss for all I cared. 'Have you?'

'I suppose the road goes straight on for Uttoxeter?' he said, when I didn't seem much interested.

'That's right.' I opened my atlas at page 148. 'Haven't you got a map?'

He pulled out a small-scale black and white thing and, looking at my single back bag, thought that some people should get their priorities right. I asked where he was going.

'I'm making for Oswestry. After Uttoxeter, it's sixty more miles.'

I was glad it was Oswestry and not Uttoxeter. You could call someone Oswestry, which even so was bad enough, but Uttoxeter would sound a bit of a mouthful, not to mention milk-soppy. On those grounds I might have taken to him a bit more if he'd come from Stoke or Crewe or even Stafford itself. Still, some people have to live in places like Oswestry or Rugeley or Uttoxeter. He ran with his bike, and leapt on as if it was a horse.

I got back on mine, and pointed my handlebars in the right direction. 'I'm going to Stafford.'

Coming level, he said: 'Do you mind if I ride with

you part of the way?'

I had too much to think about to want company, hating anyone to disturb my dreams of roaming with Alice in the gardens of Wishdale Abbey and lying down in the undergrowth to go all the way with her. Then I remembered being haunted by not knowing how the X-ray would turn out, and thought the torment of uncertainty might get so bad I'd roll under the next lorry rumbling along. On the other hand I didn't see how Oswestry on his swift model would want to slow down for a heavy one like mine made up of different bits and pieces, and supposed I would soon be riding alone anyway. 'You can if you like.'

'I assumed you were from the village, or thereabouts. That's why I asked the way.' He seemed careful not to offend me. I don't know why. He kept by my side, till a tractor honked us into single file. Then he came level again. Thick grass, orchards and wheat surrounded every farm down in the shallow valley of the River Dove. The green was as rich as if there was no other colour on earth. Clouds were piled high, cumulus with upper rims as sharp in outline as the Norfolk coast on a map. I nearly went into the verge from looking. Telling myself that I was away from home, away from the factory, and away from where no X-ray results could get at me, only reminded me of them, the last one most of all. I laughed at the idea that thinking proved I was alive, no matter what it was about. Even worry was better than nothing. 'I'll be staying a day or two in Stafford.'

'Where did you start?'

I told him.

We took a rise, and said nothing.

He was a few yards in front, but I pulled close at the top. Maybe he drew back to let me catch up. I couldn't care less. It's up to him, I said to myself. 'I left this morning, but I like going slow.'

'Why are you going to Stafford?' he wanted to know.

'For a ride,' I called from twenty yards ahead. 'It's good to be out. I'm on holiday.' That was the idea, otherwise set for nowhere in particular, except getting away. All I'd craved to do since birth was take off for anywhere as long as it was far enough. I wanted to quit my family and have time to myself. Till then I had managed no more than the odd week at cadet camp, and even then I wasn't alone, having been in a tent or barrack hut with others from the same squadron. At home there was the family, and in the factory there was my mates, so I was nowhere on my own. Soon I'd be called up for flying training, and I still wouldn't be free, but that would be all right as long as nothing was wrong with the X-ray, and I knew it couldn't be, judging by how I felt, and the fact that I hadn't coughed since last bonfire night when I ran close to drop a mattress on the flames for a gang of kids who hadn't the strength or knack to do it themselves.

Oswestry was quiet for a mile or two, and I would have kept my trap shut forever if he hadn't asked: 'Are you on holiday from school?'

'From work.' I thought it good being taken for somebody who was at grammar school, always feeling that I looked exactly what I was. I hadn't worked nearly four years in a factory to be mistaken for a schoolkid, and wanted to be seen for the way I lived. I let him catch up, and considered telling him to mind his own business. 'I volunteered in April, so I can be called up any time. I'm on reserve, and waiting for my papers.'

'I should be getting mine next spring.' He wiped a couple of gnats from his face. 'I expect I'll go into the army, even though the war is over.'

'The Japanese are still in it. If I get through training I'll be flying off aircraft carriers, because I've joined the Fleet Air Arm. I wanted to be a navigator, but they'd only take me as a pilot.'

He smiled. 'I'm all for getting in, and out, as quickly as I can. My father needs me in his office. He's a solicitor.'

As far ahead as that was a million miles away. I couldn't imagine getting to the end of my service, though I supposed it was bound to happen some day. When I was in I was in, and for all I knew about afterwards, whenever that might be, it was a concrete wall that my mind slid off, leaving me in no mood to think useless thoughts.

When I stopped at Sudbury Park, Ozzie pulled up as well. I took the small guide book from my saddlebag and flipped it open. I suppose he wondered why I had a guide book at all, but he didn't ask. A teacher at school once said that if you went travelling and wanted to know about the places you passed through you had to have a guide book, so I'd taken his advice.

'Sudbury Park is a fine Elizabethan house,' I read from the neat little book. 'Queen Adelaide lived there. The other side is a deer park.'

'You don't say?' He tried to find the subject interesting while I, without knowing why, felt like laughing at myself – or laughing at him being too well brought up to laugh at me. I could feel it, thick as butter. So that we could talk he didn't hunch forward over his racing handlebars but put both hands to the middle and sat upright, bringing us to the same level. The only sound was the steady ticking spin of the wheels, disturbed by an odd bump in the road. 'I'll get there tonight,' he said. 'Fairly late, but I'll make it.'

'You should do. But what's the hurry? You could put up somewhere on the way. I think there's a youth hostel at Shrewsbury.'

'I'm going via Stoke.'

'I don't know where I'm heading, after Stafford, but I'll be taking it easy, you can bet.'

He pointed to a patch of flowers up a grassy bank, lilac-pink heads shifting in the breeze. 'That's common mallow. Or *malva sylvestris*, if you like.'

He seemed to be on nodding acquaintance with most of the flowers we passed, from scruffy dead-nettles and creeping trefoil, to black horehound which was blue, and which I knew for a fact stank like buggery when crushed. He rattled off Latin names like music, and it was obvious he hadn't taught himself, or learned botany at evening school. 'The best flowers are gone, as far as I'm concerned,' he said. 'By the end of May, it's all over.'

I had roamed the countryside but didn't know much beyond what a cowslip or daisy looked like. You can only see what you know. If you know nothing you see nothing, just a Technicolor blur. A plane flew low and I told him it was a Liberator – four engines, big belly, twin tail – a bomber and long-range reconnaissance aircraft that looked beautiful in the blue light before vanishing into clouds. I'd passed my aircraft recognition test at ninety-two per cent, but he was one up on me, because aeroplanes change all the time, while flowers stay the same.

'Spring is the best time for flowers.' His nose started to run, and he wiped it with a folded white handkerchief. 'I love to see the first ones coming up after the winter.'

'I like the summer,' I told him. 'Sometimes I hardly notice spring. Easter's always bad for weather. I biked to the Peak District the year before last, with some pals. We set off at night, and slept in a field near Bakewell. We would have got soaked the next night, but a farmer near Chapel-en-le-Frith let us sleep in his barn. It was bloody cold, though. Last Easter I biked to the coast and slept in a pillbox near Wainfleet. Summer would have been better. I get my holidays then, and it's warmer.'.

'You should take a tent,' he said. 'You can be really warm in a tent, especially if there are two of you. Canvas holds the heat in.'

We were going up a hill so I was too puffed to answer. I wouldn't fancy sleeping in a tent with Albert, and that was a fact, though I wouldn't mind sharing one with Alice Sands. Birds were whistling on telegraph wires, as if they preferred summer as well. 'I earn six quid a week, except for tax, but you can't buy tents since the war started.'

'I've got one from before the war. It belongs to my father, really, but he lets me take it when I go camping with the Scouts. He used it all through the Great War in France, and it's still good.'

A man and woman came from the opposite direction, out for touring though they had sit-up-and-beg bikes. The woman wore a yellow frock, and the man a sports coat and cap. They waved, and we waved back. I supposed they were going to Derby, maybe to Nottingham, and then on to Skegness to lie among the dunes. Perhaps they would camp a few nights in the same machine-gun post me and Albert had slept in. It would be August in a few days, and warmer than we had it. On the other hand perhaps they were going only a mile down the road to see an aunt or a brother-in-law, though I hoped not. I liked to think that everybody was on the move and set for a long trip like I was.

'What sort of work do you do?' he wanted to know.

'I'm in a factory, on a capstan lathe.'

'Must be difficult.'

'No, it only took about a week to learn.'

'It would take me longer than that, I'm afraid.'

He must be joking, I thought. We were on a level stretch. 'Why have you got to get to Oswestry today?'

'Because we're having a party.'

'Is it a birthday?'

'Oh no. Dad and his friends are going to celebrate. He just wants me to be there. Would you like to come? They won't mind if I bring a friend.'

Maybe I would have said yes, and gone there, but it was easing too much north, and my inclination was to edge south. I would hang around Stafford as long as Alice wanted me to, even a whole week if necessary, then dash back to Nottingham to clock in at the factory on time next Monday. 'I've got to be in Stafford this afternoon.'

'A pity. You'd be welcome.'

He seemed to mean it, yet I felt he would have been a bit put out if I'd accepted his offer. 'How long's your party going to last?'

His laugh echoed a sheep which baa-ed from a field. 'All night, I believe. Maybe the whole of tomorrow. They're expecting the results of the General Election.'

'Who do they think is going to win?'

'The Conservatives, of course.'

'Do you think they will?'

'They're bound to, I should think. Father telephoned my aunt in Derby where I was staying, and said I had to be back on time.'

'I'll wait and read about it in the paper,' I said. 'Or I'll hear it on somebody's wireless. Or I won't bother. I'm on holiday.' Voting had been six weeks ago, and seemed like years. It didn't seem to matter anymore. Every week passed like a year. When voting day was over I had forgotten it had ever taken place. Work went on, and I had been looking forward to my bike trip, and to seeing Alice Sands. And here I was, going to visit her in Stafford, which was hard to believe, with Oswestry jabbering by my side. My parents had voted Labour, or so they had said. They'd been in the pub that evening and I don't think they'd bothered to vote. When I told Uncle Fred in the asylum that I hoped Labour would win he shook his head up and down and started to cry. I couldn't tell who he would have voted for. Neither Ozzie or I had voted, and that was a fact. 'If I had my way, you should be able to vote at sixteen.'

Now he was puffed out, and didn't want to talk. At least he acted like it. 'That's too young, in my opinion,' he managed to say. 'We had a debate on it at school.'

'Not for me.' I couldn't care less. It was all finished now. 'I'd know how to vote though, if I was allowed.'

The road was straight and flat, but a cyclist coming from the opposite direction was bent against the wind. 'Oh,' he said, 'I would, as well.'

After a bit of a climb through Doveridge we sailed down across the river and onto page 147 of my atlas, which took us into Staffordshire. We bumped under the railway bridge, and the streets of Uttoxeter, which we had seen from a rise two miles away, were around us. 'Do you fancy some refreshments?' Oswestry asked.

Feeling knackered, I gave him a nod, and we found an old-fashioned teashop just beyond the market place. When we settled ourselves in I asked the woman for a pot of tea and some scones. Oswestry ordered coffee and a sandwich. I stretched my legs, and looked up Uttoxeter in the guide book.

'What does it say?'

I felt a bit loony. 'Not much.'

He looked out of the window. 'Not surprising.'

The woman set our grub on the table. 'It says that Dr Johnson stood without a hat on in the rain, because he'd refused to work at his father's bookstall fifty years before.'

'You don't say?' He seemed really interested.

'Well, the book does. My old man's a cabinet-maker, but I don't want to follow in his trade.'

'It's a problem,' Ozzie said.

'Not for me.'

We wondered what the two square-headed metal things were which hung from the ceiling. I thought they were heaters, but when Oswestry asked the elderly woman in charge of the place, she told him: 'No, duck, they're gas lights.'

I closed the book and took a shilling from my pocket to pay. There was nearly a quid in change. 'Old Father Thames' was belting from the kitchen wireless. I didn't have a wallet, and three pound notes were tucked into the back page of my atlas.

'It's paid.' A fly settled on Oswestry's face, and he brushed it slowly away. He saw that I thought he had a cheek, and tried to make up. 'I did it on my way from the lavatory just now, without thinking. I hope you don't mind.' He tucked a leather purse into his back pocket. 'I'm quite well off this summer.'

I offered him a cigarette. 'So am I.'

He refused. 'Mother's made it a condition that if I don't smoke before I'm twenty-one she'll give me fifty pounds.'

'She won't know.'

'Perhaps not, but it's a point of honour.'

It was obvious I shouldn't have said it, so I stopped myself saying it again. 'Next time, everything's on me.'

33

'It's a deal, except that I think I'll smoke a pipe, if ever I do. My father does.' He laughed, and I couldn't stay mad at what he had done. 'Are you sure you won't come as far as Oswestry? It's sure to be a good party. Plenty of food and drink. They've been putting stuff by for weeks.'

'I'd like to, but I can't. I don't suppose I'll be heading in that direction for a long time.'

We shook hands, before going our different ways. He winced as if I was trying to break his fingers. Maybe I'm not used to shaking hands, I thought, but he had been the one to offer it. He leapt onto his bike like a cowboy. I waved back, remembering how we usually thumped each other on the shoulder at home, or did nothing at all. Words were enough. Sometimes not even that.

IV

My guts were in both feet on the climb out of Uttoxeter, and I pushed down for all they were worth. Knowing it would take a few days to get used to such work didn't make it any easier. In the factory I stood on one spot all day, hardly using my legs, and now it was up hill and down dale, lush parks left and right, the way slower on my own, though I'd only got fourteen miles to go. I hadn't even asked Ozzie's real name, nor had he wanted to know mine. That's how it was. 'Look me up in Oswestry,' he said, as if I'd spot him a mile off ten years from now.

'Come to Nottingham, and I'll buy you a pint in the Trip to Jerusalem.' We laughed, and drifted away. He had been friendly enough. I could only hope, though didn't, that he and his family would enjoy their party when news of the General Election came through on the wireless.

I was glad to be on my own, all the same. Why it was I don't know. When in the factory, or at home, or with my mates at the cadets, I didn't dream of getting away from them, but now I realized it was all I wanted to do.

There was nothing but trouble keeping up with someone biking by my side, or he had trouble keeping up with me. I can't stay level with anyone, but manage to be up front or behind, and feel no satisfaction unless I'm ahead, which means continual effort. I've got to be either first, or on my own, nothing else will do, if I can get away with it. When I do have company I try not to let it rile me, but at times like this I prefer to go at my own pace, slow or fast it makes no difference, my rate being the only one that matters – since I was on holiday. All the same, I was nagged that Oswestry had gone, and wanted to know more about him, now that it was too late.

Thought turned to worry, and worry to grumbling, so to stop my gallop I recalled how a few weekends ago I'd gone with my mother to see Uncle Fred at the Home he lived in. He was my father's only brother, and ten years older than him, and had been in the Home since his wife decided she'd had enough and walked out one day, though that had been only the beginning of his spin downhill.

'He's always been like that, though,' my mother said. 'You could tell he was going that way for years.' Whenever I checked my father, or did something he didn't like, he tried to frighten me by shouting: 'You'll go the same way as your Uncle-bloody-Fred if you're not careful.' There was a secret about him that neither my father or mother would tell me. I knew it, but didn't ask, or couldn't, because I sensed there was no point, and the longer this went on the less interested I became, which was maybe what everyone wanted.

Uncle Fred had always liked me, I didn't know why, and my mother had got me to go with her every couple of months to see him in the hospital-home by saying that that was the only thing she had ever asked me to do. So I went. My father hated him, couldn't be bothered to visit his own brother, which mystified me because I would never do the same to my brother. Perhaps that was why I gave in to mam, and went with her now and again to see Uncle Fred.

'It makes such a difference to him if you come for an hour,' she said. 'You've got no idea.' But I disliked the visits, because I just sat by his bed, while he looked at me and cried in silence. He'd had a stroke and couldn't talk properly, which was a pity because I always thought he wanted to tell me something important. The last time I was there a bluebottle kept landing on his forehead and he couldn't lift a hand to knock it away. It was a big and cocky fly, meaty and spiteful, and wouldn't give over harassing him.

Sitting with Fred, I sometimes felt like crying myself, when I wasn't blinding-mad at having to be there at all. Fred smiled as much as he cried, and a hand that couldn't lift to swat a fly crept out of the bedclothes, and held mine, and pressed it hard. I wanted to scat because it felt funny, another man holding my hand like that, but my mother sat on the other side of the bed, her eyes forcing me to stay, and not yank my hand away.

The bluebottle was having a field day on Fred's forehead. It took off and landed like an army-reconnaissance Lysander, and I kept thinking that Fred was trying to pass a message to me that couldn't be put into words. His hand squeezed, as if signalling, but it

36

was no good, until for some reason or other I said to myself: 'I'll get that tormenting fly. That's what he wants me to do.'

I flicked it away, and reached for a folded newspaper. Fred hated that fly for tantalizing him. He couldn't do a thing about it, though his eyes said that if he had been young and healthy, or just normally fit, it wouldn't have dared pester him. I was beginning to read him clear and simple, but it came too late.

My mother said that Fred liked me because he had known me as a baby. He used to take me out in my pram. I remembered going on a bus to Wollaton Park or up Trent Bridge, especially when it was raining. He took me on a rowing boat and bought ice cream. Fred was six feet tall and had black hair – raven black, my mother said about her brother-in-law, as if she liked no head of hair better in all the world. But now Fred's hair was grey and balding, and straggly at the back, so that I hoped one of the nurses would run the scissors round it.

Between getting flipped away from Fred's face the fly went to the window, where it stood thinking about when to make the next sortie. I could read its mind as if I was underneath those wings, and I didn't like the pest any better for that.

The story went that in those days, something funny happened to Uncle Fred. He became too lively. He went barmy, in other words. My mother said it was because of the life he had led. He'd only wanted to enjoy himself. I couldn't believe it, but she swore it was the truth. He had been married, but his wife left him. Then she died. 'Your Aunt Joyce,' my mother called her. But Fred had always been one to like women. 'He went out with a different one every night,' my mother said. 'The lucky devil,' my father added, as if he hated and admired him at the same time. He was caught at his antics, but half-killed the man, for which he spent a couple of months in prison. Next time, somebody nearly pulverized him. He would get into fights, create hell for no reason. 'I could see what was coming,' my father said, while mother looked at him and said nothing. 'He deserved all he got.'

The fly, with a joyful buzz, came back, and I hated it more than anything else in the world because it had been needling Fred for days. Maybe for weeks. It came out of its egg and said: I'll get that silly old bastard who can't defend himself. So I thought: If I kill it perhaps he'll get better. His wits'll improve. It's got to be done away with.

I made its life hell by not letting it settle even for a second, and when it flew back to the window for a rest I flitted it from there also. I gave it no peace. Fred looked at me, glad the fly was getting some of its own medicine. His eyes stopped running, and I was sure he knew what I was doing. You have it on the run, his look said. Keep it that way. So I haunted that fly by waving it off Fred's face, and away from the warm window. Fred smiled, and he hadn't done that for years, a smile of ease and sunshine.

When the fly landed on the window, I didn't touch it. The menacing, cocksure strings and wings and beady eyes seemed to breathe in and out with triumph at having worn me out, and then settled down for a well-earned rest.

With my folded newspaper lifted and ready, I batted that tormenting bluebottle as no other bluebottle had been batted in the history of the world.

At least Fred thought so. He started twitching, his hands shaking, and eyes all a-wink when I knocked the dead mess onto the floor. My mother heard the bang, and came back from talking to the nurse. I felt as if I had committed murder. Whether it was against the fly or against Fred I didn't know – or even against myself. She told me to stop larking about, with a look as if she wanted to knock me flat for what I had done, and I didn't know what that was anymore. She clearly wondered why Uncle Fred was laughing, when I hadn't heard such a pleasant sound from him for ages.

He kept on laughing till his face changed colour, and when the ward sister and a male nurse came in they shooed us away and put screens round his bed because what had started as a laugh turned into a heart-attack death-rattle.

'Well, it had to come some time,' my father said later, but I sat two hours in the waiting-room, and even now couldn't remember whether everything was painted dark green above the brown skirting-board, or whether the skirting-board was painted green below the dark brown walls. I don't think I knew at the time, what's more. The fact that Uncle Fred was dying blunted my ability to take things in.

Visiting hour was over and I was the only one left. A nurse sent a ward maid out with a cup of tea. I had to go to Crewe next morning, to the aircrew selection board of the Royal Navy, and could only think of the questions they were going to ask. Uncle Fred would either live or die, and I considered I had already done my best for him, or worst. As I sat there I knew myself to be at the middle of a disaster that I could do nothing about, never thinking I was the one who had set it going.

I missed the funeral, and still haven't been to the grave, but hoped I would before joining up and leaving the place for good. When everyone was setting off for the graveyard I sat rooted to the settee in the parlour, but at the last minute, as the cars were lining up out-side, I pushed between my mother and Aunt Millie, and went out of the house. I walked about downtown till I knew they were back from the cemetery, and even the party was over. I expected my mother never to talk to me again, but whether she understood or not, she never mentioned what I had done. Even my father went to the funeral, though it nearly choked him.

V

I leaned my bike against a park wall, and opened the guide book to read that Loxley was the place where Robin Hood was born. I'd never thought that 'Robbin' bastard', as we called him at work, was real, but I was happy to learn something new, especially from a sixpenny book picked up off a stall. I wondered how Robin Hood had got to Nottinghamshire from Loxley, to begin his antics against the sheriff and his men. I could only suppose he had made his way across country like a fugitive, going from one patch of forest to the next, living off berries and cherries and poachers' meat. He must have swam the Trent one dark night with an arrow between his teeth, and one of his earrings going rusty. When he got to Sherwood he met somebody else and started a gang. Forty miles was a lot of landscape in those days.

I balanced my book on the saddle while eating a cheese sandwich. It was stale because I'd packed it the night before, but it tasted no less juicy. Being my first bite since breakfast, except for the fluffball scones in Uttoxeter, I was famished.

A man on a horse came out of the park gates and went across the road to a lane entrance. He wore a smart hat and leggings, and certainly had a good view of the countryside, though he looked half asleep, as if he didn't care what took place round him, though I supposed that if he saw Robin Hood (bastard or not) emerging from one of his coppices, he would take a pocket pistol (silver) from under his long coat and shoot him dead. He wore leather gloves, and had a white flower in his buttonhole, which almost glittered when set against his face of beetroot red. Maybe he was also off to a party, to wait for when the election news came through.

When he was a little way up the lane he turned round, as if he had forgotten something. I thought he hadn't seen me, or was too high and mighty to notice, but he looked for a moment or two, and then called out across the road: 'Take your cycle away from that wall.'

Stiffening my back, I looked around as if to see who he meant.

'And don't leave it there again.'

I had been about to go, anyway.

'Or you'll be in trouble, let me tell you.'

I didn't mind being told what to do in the factory, because it was necessary to get things done. Being ordered about on cadet parades so as to learn something, and as preparation for being in full-time service, was what I had volunteered for. But to be spoken to in such a way by that bastard, though I wasn't aware of doing any harm at all, caused a flash of rage to send me over the top, especially when he rattled on with:

'What's your name?'

'Robin Hood!' I told him, in my loudest parade-ground voice.

He looked much less sleepy as his face twitched from red to purple. 'Wait!' he called, in a voice gone squeaky.

'Stay where you are.'

'Bollocks,' I shouted.

I heard the hooves move, and a sound as of the horse throwing snot from its nostrils, so I turned and leapt onto my saddle, imitating Ozzie sooner than I'd thought. Fortunately it was first-time luck, because I landed squarely, realizing that both man and beast were out to get me.

He ranted something, or maybe called for assistance in the last round-up. My brain was empty, yet it warned me away from the main road where everything could be seen for miles. My bike did a quick conversion to a Mustang, and I switched left onto a minor road that went by the park, and then veered into no-man's land.

The lane ascended. I put all my force to the pedals because hooves were clip-clopping behind. It wasn't terror, more like an orderly panic and, meeting level ground, I put a rocket at my crossbar, by which time the man's curses faded, the ripe ones as if he had heard them in his cradle and learned a few juicier ones since, proving him to be one of Robin Hood's descendants who had made friends with the barons and built his fortune up.

I spun the tale through long and desperate pedalling until the lane sloped down, fleeing in a fair fight between horse and bike on a tarmacadamed road. Never looking back, almost sick with keeping such an effort up, I forked right, went by a mill over a stream, and took another hill, fleeing as if all Staffordshire was out for my guts.

At the top of the hill I pulled up by a coppice, and found a stone by the laneside in case the man on the horse was loony enough to stay on my trail, determined he would be the first to bleed, whoever he was. If he guessed what I was thinking he would come no closer, though I didn't suppose he could be bothered after losing sight of me.

I took out my trusty atlas, and stretching my legs and opening it on my knees, saw that by going through Hixon and crossing the Trent to Tixall I could get into Stafford without returning to the main road, thus following a foolproof parallel route. Or I would carry on from Tixall, go down to Milford on the Rugeley road, and approach Stafford from another direction altogether. Such a way would take longer, but was less boring than sticking to the route I'd planned.

I laughed aloud at the fact that I hadn't been three years in the Cadets and learned map-reading for nothing, though on this diversion I felt myself going almost blind looking through the small print to find the lanes. I also had to change pages of the atlas – the more pages the better – but even the map was edging me into a corner as I flipped from page 147 to page 127 and back again.

I let my breath become easy, and decided to celebrate my escape by smoking a fag. I also supposed it would calm me. Putting a hand in my pocket for the cigarettes, I thought to read a bit from my guide book to see if any of the new villages I would go through were mentioned. Part of my holiday was to make headway, but not hurry. All day at the factory was like one rushing drumbeat after another to get my stint done. My father called me at half past six, and I left the house an hour later to cycle three miles so as to clock in by eight. At dinnertime I ran half a mile to the canteen and ate quickly so as to have twenty minutes playing tincan football in the street with my mates. I went full tilt at my machine till five, then cycled home as fast as I could. On two nights I went to classes at the Cadets, on others I studied or went for a long bike ride. Or I had a date with Janice. There wasn't a minute to spare. That was how I liked it, but now that I was on holiday I wanted to treat myself to slowing down whenever I felt like it.

The guide book wasn't there. I searched through the bag twice. I spread everything on the grass, then quickly repacked it in case Sir Robin Hood should appear. The book must have slipped out in my hurry to escape. It served me right, but the loss almost brought tears to my eyes. With two more stones in my pocket I wanted to go back, and find it. I longed for the Short Lee Enfield high-powered long-range .303 rifle which I had fired at annual camps, as I piston-legged as far as the mill, determined to fight the whole world for my book.

I stopped, and mulled on the proceedings as a story for Alice Sands, wondering whether she would laugh when I told her. A magpie was strafing the lane. I watched water racing between reeds under the bridge, minnows and sticklebacks lamping their way through. I was dazed by water as it swept along. If I searched for my book by the park wall, and the man tried to stop me (I saw it happening in the moving glass of the water) and I threw stones, and one hit him at the temple, as with David against Goliath in the Bible, I wouldn't become king but would be hanged in Stafford jail. Then I would have no story to tell, not to Alice anyway.

But there were always two pictures. Maybe me and the man on the horse would laugh at the sight of each other as we rounded the same corner and pulled up sharp, and think what a funny world it was that we had entered into a competition over such a trivial matter. And then we would shake hands and he would invite me to the house for a drink and something to eat before

44

showing me on my way: 'Call again, when you happen to be passing.'

'Do you mean that?'

'Any time. I like a young chap who shows he's not afraid of anything.'

'All right, Loxley.'

'Don't forget. Come any time. There are no hard feelings on my side.'

Not much, I supposed. But maybe that conversation would make just as good a yarn, both of them unlikely, and I didn't know which one she would like best. For some reason I remembered being at the aircrew selection board and reading upside down what was written on my enrolment form. It made a picture as others saw me, information saying that my hair was brown, my eyes blue-grey, my complexion fresh, and that for distinguishing marks I had several moles at the back of the neck. These, I told myself, were probably big blackheads caused by the oily air of the factory, things which the naval doctor had never seen in his life. My height was given as five feet eight inches, though I hoped I'd put on a bit since then, though my 140 pounds weight must have been more or less the same.

It seemed irrelevant. I didn't care how I looked to the world, because I had passed the intelligence and aptitude tests, which pleased me most of all. To find that I had got perfect health and eyesight was satisfying, but to go back to the Cadet squadron sporting a white flash in my cap showing that I'd squeezed through the selection board exams, the goal of everyone who joined and which few achieved, was what I had lived for but never dreamed I would get.

Who was I to worry about a lunatic on a horse? Full of optimism and well being, I didn't even think I had TB. I would meet Alice Sands in an hour or two, and we would walk arm in arm through the gardens of Wishdale Abbey, and then in a dry spot get down to kissing, which would lead to the best thing of all. Smiling at such a prospect, I dropped each stone into the tail of the one in front, concentric circles in the water like the illustrations of waves coming from radio aerials.

With lighter pockets I cycled back up the hill. Nobody would find me in this maze of lanes. If I went fast enough in circles I would hardly be able to find myself, which at the moment didn't bother me. A good thing about being on my own was the knowledge that if there had been two of us, one might have been caught. I wouldn't have acted so quickly in the complicated getaway. Neither, I suppose, would I have been so hasty in chelping Horseback Henry by the manor wall, who had perhaps found the guide book with my name and address written in it. Much good may it do him. For all I cared he could keep it for ever and ever, though I expect he chucked it in a dustbin.

VI

I shoved my tuppence in, dialled, and pressed Button A when a man asked what I wanted.

'Does Alice Sands live there?'

'She did – up to just now. She might still, for all I know.'

Funny. 'Can I speak to her, please?'

'You can.'

'Thanks.' Then I kept quiet and waited.

He turned gruff, as if he'd got his troubles. 'I'll find out whether she'll speak to you.' Words cost money in these parts. Alice came on. I could tell her voice: 'Who is it?'

'Paul. I'm in Stafford.' The booth steamed up in expectation, though her tone didn't bring back the face I had been seeing on my ride from Nottingham. Her voice was flat, and didn't seem very interested, but I supposed it was bound to seem fed up if the man who had spoken first had been her father.

'What about Albert?'

I told her he'd fallen off his bike last night and scraped the side of his face. 'A real mess, it was.'

'That's too bad.'

'He went to the hospital to get it treated in case he got lockjaw. He came back bandaged as if he'd caught mumps. He had five – no, six – injections.'

I felt ashamed of lying, but there was nothing I could do. In any case it did no harm. Maybe she wouldn't bring Gwen now, and we would be on our own.

'Are you going back today?'

'I've got no lamps on my bike.' It was true, but I might have lied even if it hadn't been. 'I wouldn't get back till midnight. But I've also got a whole week off work, so I might stay a day or two around Stafford. It's a nice place.'

'I'd like to meet you, then.'

'I've been looking forward to it.' I tried not to sound sarky.

'So have I.'

That was an improvement.

'Where are you going to stay tonight?'

'In a ditch,' I said, 'if I can find one vacant.'

She laughed.

'I'll get bed and breakfast. There's bound to be one in the town.' I'd done my share, and wouldn't speak till she said something. I didn't like telephoning, not having done much before, except to find out how Uncle Fred was at the hospital. I preferred to see who I was talking to, not listen to a ghost voice coming out of a bakelite cup, and having to imagine what the eyes said and how the lips moved, and whether the person was picking their nose or not. I'd never get used to it.

'Did you have a good trip from Nottingham?'

'It was all right.'

'I hope you did.'

'I'll tell you when I see you.' The pause was so long I could have spun my whole life story in it. 'When will you be coming into town?'

'I'll call for Gwen,' she said, 'and we'll catch the next bus. We can meet in front of the post office.'

'When will that be?'

'In an hour.'

I pressed Button B, and let a woman waiting outside with two crying kids go in the box. She had dried blood on her lips, and a black eye, and said she had come to phone the police station. Holding the door open, I pointed to her bruised face.

'Who did that?'

'My husband.'

She was tall, a strong-looking but gaunt woman, and wore a velvet hat. Her thin hair was going grey. Both the kids were boys, and I hoped they would soon grow up so that they could frighten him to death. 'You should kick his teeth in,' I said, leaving her to it.

I rode down the street, thinking about how during a big argument, just before Uncle Fred went into the Home, when it looked as if my father would kick my mother, she snatched up a heavy poker and took a swipe at him. The stubby end went only an inch from his nose, but he staggered back, and never threatened her again. One of Albert's aunts whose husband came

out of jail and started knocking her about got the
boiling teapot thrown at him, and you can still see the
scar, though they don't argue anymore, at least not loud
enough for anybody to hear. When he was led to the
hospital, moaning, with a towel over his face and a
lighted fag sticking through the hole he told the doctor
he had been painting a table leg and the teapot fell on
him when he accidentally pulled at the newspaper it
stood on. But most men get away with thumping their
wives.

Veering off the main road, I saw a big house with a
sign by the garden wall saying TEMPERANCE HOTEL.
I banged the black knocker, and a man in shirtsleeves
opened the glass-panelled door of many colours. 'What
is it you want?'

My impulse was to say I had seen all those lovely
brand new racing bikes in his shop window, and what
was the asking price for the one with the pink and
yellow ribbons fastened on its handlebars? What did
you knock at a hotel door for? But I leaned my bike by
the steps and asked Joseph if I could stay there for the
night.

'Cost you four-and-a-tanner. Breakfast thrown in,
though.'

I wondered what the rate would have been for two
people, but didn't ask, because Alice Sands would never
do a thing like that. My cousin had taken a woman to a
bed-and-breakfast place for the night and it had cost
six-and-sixpence each. And they didn't get any breakfast. 'That'll be all right,' I told him.

'In advance.' He asked to see my Identity Card, and
I showed him.

'Where can I leave my bike?'

He looked at it, and smiled. 'Round the back. I'll
show you.' A rickety gate opened into a garden

overgrown with brambles and elderberry bushes. He pointed to a shed full of broken plant pots and rolls of oil cloth. I just about got the back wheel in, and when I pulled the door to he locked it. One good kick and the door would be off its hinges. Another shove, and it would be flat, with my bike underneath. 'I'll show you where you can sleep.'

I followed him into the house and up a flight of dusty stairs. The billet was fair enough, so I paid the money. There was a single bed in the room as well as a double one, and I wondered which of the two I would use. Looking out of the window, I saw a lorry driving down the street with so much smoke coming from its tail that I thought it would burst into flames.

The single bed folded me into a hammock when I tried it, and I had to fight my way clear. The springs of the double bed creaked but at least stayed flat when I lay full length, so I decided to sleep on that. I had a good wash in the bathroom, though I'd steamed-and-cleaned myself at the public baths only the day before. At the third try the parting in my hair came straight. I even got a bit of a quiff, so with the cape folded under my arm in case it rained, I went back to the middle of town, glad my lodgings were settled at least.

There was time to spare so I went into a stationer's to buy a manual on how to recognize flowers in the countryside. After hearing Oswestry rattle off their names I thought I would learn to do the same. The book had plenty of coloured pictures, so it wouldn't be hard. The shop girl stood close, while I looked through the book to make sure it was good enough. She wore a brown frock with cloth-covered buttons right down the middle, and her fair hair was in a roll around her forehead. From flipping the pages, I looked at her.

She smiled. 'Is it all right, then?'

'Yes. It'll do.' I wondered what she would say if I asked her for a date, but I didn't in case she said yes, because if she did, where would I be with Alice Sands? 'How much is it?'

'Half a crown.' She wore lipstick, had nylon stockings on, and smelled of scent, but her figure wasn't very good. I would have liked a date with her, all the same. Alice today, and her tomorrow. Albert would have gone blue with envy. But it was too good to come true.

I asked if they had a street plan of Stafford. I always felt pleasure, almost achievement, to see where I was on a map. If I saw where I belonged on a map I belonged more to myself, and also knew better than my own sense where I was in the world. All she could offer was the coloured sheet of the Ordnance Survey for one-and-sixpence. She apologized for it being paper-flat instead of on cloth, but I was glad to have it, thinking you still needed police permission to buy this kind of map. You did in Nottingham, anyway, unless it was only black and white, though things might have altered now that the war in Europe was over.

She smiled as I went off with my trophies, and I waved to her from the door. Reading the map as I went up the street, I saw that though Stafford was stuck in one corner, it showed the area of the aerodrome where I had been at cadet camp with Albert. I also noticed, while standing by the post office waiting for Alice, that the grounds of Wishdale Abbey were marked as well.

VII

The time went too quickly.

'Paul Morton!'

I looked up, folded the map, and put it in my pocket. Warm dry lips touched mine for a second. She wore a soft mackintosh and belt, and a beret which made her face look thinner and almost caused the freckles to disappear. Her kiss smelled of roses, and there was the garden of Wishdale Abbey in each hazel eye. That's what I'd hoped; but there wasn't. She was a stranger to me. If she hadn't shouted my name I wouldn't have recognized her. I couldn't believe I'd seen her before, though I kept hold of her arm till she drew away.

'I'm glad you came back,' she said. 'I liked getting your letters.'

I'd put a lot into them, written them out over and over again. 'And I liked yours.'

She looked down. 'I'm sorry Albert didn't come. Or Gwen is. It's a shame.'

I wondered how long it would be before the strato-cumulus cloud shook out some rain. Or maybe it would blow over, though it hardly ever did. 'Maybe she won't miss much.'

She gave me a sharp nudge. 'You know what I mean.'

Albert was innocent of any crime, but I donned a black cap for him at that moment. He would have done the same if I hadn't wanted to come. By my side he would have been worth his weight in gold.

The green floorcloth of a bus hid Gwen, who stood on the corner. I was glad she had let Alice come across to greet me alone. All the same, I hoped she would get swallowed up.

'We'd better go to her,' Alice said.

The well-buttoned maroon coat made Gwen seem stout. She looked older. But I wanted to draw my fingers along her full face to see if the skin was real. She had wonderful skin, like gloss on rose petals, though it was halfway spoiled by her sulky expression at how things had turned out. I found later that I was wrong. She didn't care about Albert. She just didn't want Alice to meet me, and was mad that she had, because it meant as far as Gwen was concerned that she had to waste her own half-day and evening coming with Alice. Perhaps she thought I might turn out to be dangerous. That's what went through my mind, anyway, when I wondered why she had come at all.

'Gwen's my guardian angel.' Alice's lips were about to part with laughter. I didn't think she needed one, though if so I'd be friendly with whoever took her part – except that I recognized sarcasm when I heard it.

Gwen said hello as if she wanted me to get swallowed up as well. We'd have met halfway to the middle of the earth. She reeked of scent, as if she wanted to hide the fact that she worked all week in a wet-fish shop. When she came close and asked about Albert I had to explain again why he hadn't come, feeling even more let down than when he had first told me, and unable to understand why he hadn't stuck to his promise. It seemed now that I hadn't tried very hard to make him change his mind, probably because I'd thought that if I came on my own Alice would meet me alone, and it would be easier for me to do what I wanted. I had played my cards right, but ended with the wrong ones anyway.

I couldn't tell whether Gwen was really upset about Albert breaking his promise. She didn't speak, and if people don't talk you don't know what to think. And when she did say something it was first one thing and then the other, so that I felt baffled, which might have been what she wanted, though it didn't do her much good, either. If I had been able to read her mind I didn't think I would have been any the wiser. If she had felt really bad she wouldn't have come into Stafford to see me, unless she felt more for Alice than both of us, and was only there to keep an eye on her. I wished she hadn't because there was no going back, and here she was, making it hard for me to tell Alice how much I loved her.

We wandered along Green Gate Street, plenty of people about, so that when we split up Alice walked sometimes with me and sometimes with Gwen. Or Gwen walked sometimes on her own and sometimes with Alice. It began to seem stupid, the three of us walking up and down the street saying nothing, till I was glad to feel a few drops of rain and could say it was about time we went into a café.

They said they would love to have some tea, and I felt like the good shepherd. At the table I told them everything that had happened since setting out that morning, spinning the yarn at how I swore at Horseback Henry by Loxley Hall, though careful not to bring out the actual words I had used.

'It served him right,' said Alice.

'I know. But when I escaped his clutches I lost my guide book. I'll have to buy another, if I can find one.'

They thought it was a scream, me having a guide book, and when Gwen stopped laughing she said she was surprised at me having come such a long way on my own.

'Alice was expecting me.'

This reason carried no weight at all, and for a moment I hated her, and wanted to clock her one. But Alice's smile, and the touch of her warm hand on mine, made the fifty miles worthwhile. 'I was waiting for you,' she said.

I'd have ridden a hundred and fifty. 'I like to keep a promise.'

'Well,' Gwen said, 'you promised to bring Albert, didn't you?' She couldn't have cared less, but kept on needling me about it. She wanted a bit of fun, and who could blame her? I wished she wouldn't keep having it with me, though.

A couple of tables away sat a woman wearing a hat with a bit of fur dangling from it. People had to dress in whatever they could get, with clothes being on Coupons. She lit a fag from the stub of one just smoked. It wasn't always easy to get cigarettes, either, but I supposed she rationed herself to so many a day, and hadn't smoked for a week because she'd had a cold, and now had so many in reserve that she could chainsmoke for a while. On the other hand, she didn't want to finish her tea, because then she wouldn't have an excuse to sit there. She was split between enjoying it hot, then going out into the rain, or watching it get cold, with the bonus of staying dry. I felt sorry for her.

'If you'd brought Albert,' Gwen was saying, 'we'd have had a foursome.' He isn't a slave, I thought, or a bloody parcel to be tucked under my arm. And if Albert had come without me, instead of the other way round, I wondered whether Alice would have kicked up such a fuss. I was about to say he had been absolutely too knackered to come, and that was a fact, because these days he was getting all he wanted from his sweetheart. 'He's done for,' I said. 'Didn't I tell you?'

'You could have said you weren't coming, in that case.'

What I should have said, and I thought that was what she wanted me to say with all her heart, was that Albert had made it up with his sweetheart, that at this moment he was in her parlour, that he'd got his trousers down, and she had got her knickers off, and they were sporting around on the hearthrug. 'I could,' I answered, 'but I didn't want to.'

'If I'd been you,' she said, 'I'd have been lonely, biking on my own for fifty miles.'

Alice looked as if she would slaughter her if she carried on much longer. 'He's here, isn't he?'

There was nothing to do but laugh. 'On my way I met a man coming back from Cannock Chase with twelve dead rabbits slung over his crossbar. He said his wife had sent him out to get breakfast. He'd come in drunk the night before, after spending all his wages in the boozer. I noticed a wart on his nose that he kept dabbing with a piece of cloth. When he wanted a smoke he took a cigarette case from under his cap. He said there was a hole in his head from the First World War, and it slotted in nicely. I noticed it was a silver cigarette case, though it was full of Woodbines and not Senior Service. He was standing outside a church. Then I rode ten miles with a youth who was going to Oswestry.'

'I've got an aunt in Oswestry.' Gwen was neutral for once, and I wished she had a fat and jolly aunt in every place. She even smiled because I was trying to make up for the bad time she tried to kid me she was having.

'When I stopped at a pub for a shandy,' I said, 'I got talking to a young couple who were running away from home. They were going to Skegness. Or was it Mablethorpe? Anyway, the girl said she would get a job slaving in a boarding house, and the man would work at pulling barbed wire up from the beaches. They're clearing 'em now that the war's over and nobody wants to invade anymore. Mind you, he was a bit weedy, and wasn't cut out for that sort of work, but I expect he'll get used to it. Everybody does, if they've got to.'

Alice looked, didn't know whether to believe me or not, but at least she liked talk better than silence, for she made a sign with her lips. With me it was the other way round and, surprised at jabbering so long, I wondered if I would be able to keep the tale going. 'They couldn't have been much more than eighteen, the pair of them, and they didn't look very happy, let me tell you. She was crying, and wanted to turn back. The last thing I saw, they were going off on their tandem towards Derby. They'd already come from Stoke-on-Trent. I felt sorry for them, but I expect they'll be all right in the end. I'd like to know what'll happen to them, but don't suppose I ever shall, worse luck.'

'They sound as daft as they come,' Gwen commented.

'People aren't as sensible as you,' I told her. 'Some get carried away. A friend of mine's been engaged since he was sixteen. Every night after work he has a wash, changes his clothes, and goes to his lady love's house. They sit by the fire, just looking at each other, holding hands. When I asked him what they talked about he said: "Nothing at all. But we love each other." '

Alice took off her beret. 'In't it awful?'

I wondered if she was courting, and saw myself kicking the guts out of whoever she went with. Then I saw that he had an amiable face and wore glasses, and had been to grammar school. He'd read a few books and knew some French, so we got talking and I liked him, because he was different to the rest of the people I knew, and had something interesting to say. All the same, I didn't know whether or not to kick his head in. Of course, he might have kicked mine in first. Then I thought maybe she isn't courting anyway. 'What do you do with yourself at the farm?'

'I listen to the wireless,' she said, after thinking about it. 'But there's nearly always something to do. I have to weed the garden, do the shopping, wash up, boil the clothes on Monday.' She laughed, and I wondered if it was true. 'Sometimes I go to the pictures. Or long walks with Gwen.'

I caught something between them, I didn't know what, maybe an intercepted smile, perhaps a sly look when I was half-turned to see how the woman with the cold cup of tea was getting on. 'Both of us are nearly always busy,' said Gwen.

They had a secret, for sure. Did they think I had no sense? Or did they imagine they were too cunning for me to notice? Or did they want me to notice so that they could see how I handled my bad luck? Whatever they were up to, I wasn't the only bloke Alice knew, and if that was so I don't suppose she thought I was up to much. But she wasn't the only girl I knew either, though she happened to be the one I was in love with.

'I sometimes do so much weeding,' she said, 'that when I go to bed I see weeds in front of my eyes all night. Nothing but weeds. I'm swimming and walking through them. They look better in dreams, though.' She looked as if she was still in a dream till she said: 'I like eating the lettuces and carrots when they come up. I have to clean out the chickens as well, and the rabbits.'

I was beginning to feel sorry, though she didn't look as if she was being worked half to death. I'd never had to do anything at home, except errands. The first time I sewed a button on was at cadet camp. But then, I worked all day in a factory.

They finished their tea and I got out my cigarettes. Gwen didn't smoke. 'My father shot two pigeons this morning,' Alice said, taking the one I offered, 'and I plucked them. They were fat.' I struck a match because her fag went out. She wasn't used to it. 'He shoots rabbits, but we get fed up with them. My mother does, anyway. She has to skin them, and when they was shot in the rain they stink like cats, she says.'

'I nearly ran over a cat at Mickleover.' I blew my smoke away. 'A big black one with pink eyes. I'm glad I didn't, or I might have had bad luck. I might not have got here.'

The waitresses were friendly, and called out at people from behind the tea urns, as if they'd known them or their families for years. Stafford seemed a small and homely place. Even three rowdy youths who came in and said they wanted a date with the waitresses didn't get their goat. 'I'm old enough to be your mother,' one of them shouted across.

'I don't care,' the youth said. 'I still love you, duck.'

She smiled at the compliment. 'Would you believe it?'

'You should smack his bum,' the other waitress said. 'He's a cheeky devil.' He had a quiff, and one of his mates pushed it flat for a lark, saying that otherwise if he fell down he would cut his throat on it. Gwen stared, and one of them called, as he ran a comb through his hair: 'Seen all, duck?'

She turned back to me. 'What's it like, working in a factory?'

'It's all right. I'm on a lathe.'

'Don't you get tired?'

'Not much.'

'I would.'

'You soon get used to it. Some women in our factory work on lathes, but small ones, and they've got stools to sit on.'

'Are you going to do it all your life?'

'I will if I like. But I don't expect so.'

Alice broke the cigarette in two. 'Why don't you leave him alone?'

I was beginning to think Gwen was one of those women who, as I'd heard my mother say, treated herself soft but others hard. Yet I liked her because she was taking an interest in me. She might hate me, but I could defend myself when I had to. In any case I felt that somewhere in her there was generosity, and though it wasn't very obvious I sensed it wouldn't be far away. 'I'm joining up soon,' I said.

But she wouldn't let go. 'And then what?'

I acted puzzled. 'And then what what? I don't get it.'

She leaned close. 'After you've joined up, and you come out, what will you do then? You're bound to come out one day, aren't you?'

'Maybe I'll sign on, for seven and five. You never know. There are worse things. But I don't think much about what's going to happen to me.'

'Why don't you? You're a human being, aren't you?'

I laughed at such baby talk. 'I think so. But I've got better things to do than worry about things like that.'

'Men do sign on.'

I wondered whether Alice could see I didn't like her taking my part. She had no need to rush in and defend me. I didn't altogether know what Gwen was on about either. Or I did, but it certainly had no importance. I had a job. I earned good money. I would join up and become a pilot. That was enough to be going on with. Everybody joined up, anyway. They had to. And that seemed to be the end of it. But not everybody got into aircrew. There was nothing better to aim for, and I'd got my foot in the door, even though I didn't know how wide it would open when I was allowed to go through.

'I've applied for a new job, anyway, with the Ministry of Aircraft Production.' They weren't interested, though it was the truth. It was no use boring them. The letter to say whether or not I had got the post hadn't come before I left. 'I'll only earn half the wages I'm getting now, but it'll be better work for me.

I'll get my pay every month.'

'Wages aren't everything,' Alice said.

She was right, unless you had a family to keep, but I liked earning six pounds a week in the factory. It was almost as much as the old man brought home. 'If I get the new job I'll be working in a control tower on an airfield.'

'It sounds all right,' she said.

'I've always been interested in that. Anyway, it's only temporary, until I get my papers.' Perhaps because I wanted to make them think better of me, I said, without knowing why, or even whether I was serious or not: 'But I'll never work in a factory again. All that'll be finished.'

As soon as I'd spoken I had a feeling that it would turn out to be true. I was calm about it, and didn't even think it necessary to say any more, having no one to convince.

'You can never tell, though, can you?' Gwen piped up.

'Let's go to the pictures.' I had nothing else to offer. Or I couldn't be bothered to think of anything, as if I was tired. It was hard to remember when I'd talked so openly about my life, though I often thought about it to myself. 'We can't sit here all night.'

Gwen smirked as if to say: 'Hark at him, ordering us about. Who does he think he is?' Perhaps she wasn't feeling well because of her periods. A girl I knew got a backache every time she had the rags on. Then again, maybe she was always like that. I was fed up, wishing I hadn't come, and wondering whether I shouldn't leap onto my bike and ride off towards Lichfield. It would be light for a few hours yet, and the thought of a shower of rain didn't bother me. If I hadn't paid for my night's lodging I would have done.

Alice reached over and stroked my face. 'I'd love to.'

I held her hand and kissed each finger, and she didn't draw back. Her reddish hair was soft, and fell between my fingers when I touched her warm ear. 'Let's go to Wishdale Abbey tomorrow.' Maybe I had come all this way to smell the roses and walk in the overgrown gardens, even if only on my own. Seeing Alice was a bonus, but it wasn't everything.

'You can't get in there anymore.' Gwen thought we were as daft as schoolkids for holding hands. 'They've got a fence around the place because it's going to be rebuilt.'

'That won't stop me getting in.'

'Well, somebody got in last month and walked along the rafters near the roof. He fell and broke his neck. Some people are born stupid. There's a nightwatchman living in the cottage, to keep people out.'

I didn't believe her. There wasn't a cottage close enough to be used as a guardhouse. I would see for myself, in any case. 'Maybe he wanted to get as high up off the ground as he could. Some people like to.'

'I suppose they do.' She spoke as if they were the lowest of the low.

The woman in the fur hat looked towards the window, as if she was frightened to go outside in case she met someone who would do her harm. Then again, maybe she was waiting for her husband. She stared at me, so I turned away. Did she wonder what I was doing in here with two girls? I was beginning to wonder myself.

'I suppose if I had to watch somebody climbing on the roof of the Abbey,' Alice said, 'I'd wet myself. I might like him, though, if he was up there doing it for me.'

'You wouldn't say so if you had a brother like our Ronald,' said Gwen.

I asked what was wrong with him.

'Oh nothing, nothing at all. He's just been in a wheelchair since he was ten because he fell out of a tree. That's all.'

I thought she was about to cry. 'I'm sorry.'

'I take him out sometimes, don't I?' Alice put in. 'He's not right in the head anymore,' she whispered to me.

'I heard that,' Gwen said, half-threatening, half-tearful.

'Well, it's the truth. It isn't his fault.'

'I know, but you don't need to tell all the world.'

The woman had a sallow face, though she wasn't thin. She had fair hair and dark eyes, as far as I could see. Maybe she'd had mental trouble, because there was something strange about her looks, as if she might get up and start throwing cups around the place. But the waitresses didn't think so. They were used to her. One of them brought her another cup of tea and I swear she didn't pay for it. Perhaps she was the waitress's sister, though she didn't look it. I didn't know why I thought all this. She was still close enough to her mental trouble to worry about it coming back. I thought I'd better not look at her again.

'I'd have brought a pair of wire-cutters, if I'd known the place was going to be fenced off.'

Gwen looked as if I would, wouldn't I? I was just that sort of person, wasn't I? Of course, I'd come from the right kind of place, hadn't I? God blimey, I decided, I won't mention it again, and I won't say much else, either.

'I'm sorry I didn't tell you in a letter,' Alice said. 'I didn't think.'

'We must be able to get in.'

'You can't, though.' Gwen was glad of the fact. It

63

was the best thing that had happened this year, VE Day included. 'And what do you keep looking at that woman for?'

'I don't know.' Why should I know? An airman came in and sat at her table because there was no other space. I didn't care about not being able to get into the Abbey gardens. Alice didn't want to, in any case. Maybe it would happen another year – or never – though who could tell? I'd be able to get to Wishdale Abbey every year of my life, even when I was in the Fleet Air Arm. I could go there when I was on leave, and walk around on my own, and smell the roses, and think of all the things that hadn't happened, though maybe Alice would come with me when I was a pilot. 'Who lives there?'

'Some private people bought it, but they haven't moved in yet. It's too wrecked. That's why nobody in the government wants the place anymore.'

The airman must have asked for two wads and char, because the waitress took cake and two cups on her tray. The woman was acting as if she'd never had mental trouble. She was eating, drinking, talking, telling him something, maybe her life story. Perhaps she had been a bit crackers. But she was smiling as well, almost as if he was her brother. She even took her hat off and smoothed her hair.

'She soon picked somebody up.' Gwen's voice was as loud as a foghorn and I wanted to biff her. The woman must have heard. 'He looks nice, as well.'

'What time do the pictures begin in this place?' I stood up so as to get them outside before there was a barney.

Alice looked at her wristwatch. 'Oh, we'll have to run. The little picture's already started.'

VIII

I rinsed the fish and chip smell off my fingers, then lay on the bigger bed before getting undressed. Two could have got into it, and Alice would have been just right. At home I slept with my younger brother. I would get lost in this on my own.

After the fish and chip supper, Gwen and Alice caught the last bus home. We'll see you tomorrow, and go to the Castle, Gwen said. I couldn't have cared less. You'd better get a move on, the conductor called. They wouldn't even sit on the back row in the pictures. With Gwen in between I was hardly close enough to smell her powder.

A car went by, and a light came down the wall like a knife set on cutting my throat. It wouldn't have mattered. I took my shoes and trousers off, and got into bed, trying to find a part that wasn't damp. I couldn't think what I was doing here, in this bed, at this time, why Stafford and not another place was around my neck. I'd got here under my own propulsion to keep an appointment made weeks ago, and was glad I had. But nothing had come of it.

At the same time it was hard to know, now that it had happened, what exactly it had been that I had wanted to happen. Well, I knew. I'd had girls all the way already, and that was what I wanted with Alice, but I should have known it wouldn't happen because that was never how things worked, though I always hoped they would. If I tried to make something happen it didn't, and if I didn't expect anything to happen, it did. When something happens in a natural way – but unexpected so that I don't have the pleasure of looking forward to it – that's good, but not all that good, not anywhere near as good as when I plan and hope and wait for something and it actually does come about. Yet that had never really happened, so how did I know? I didn't, but if I felt it, then there must be something to it. The only question was: Would I ever know? Would I recognize an event, if it happened, as easily as I named any type of aircraft coming through the sky, or as easily as Oswestry had labelled flowers? My spotting ability was a hundred per cent, but I was beginning to think that recognizing aeroplanes wasn't enough.

Another thing I knew was that though I was in love with Alice, or thought I was, if she had had an accident while cutting up lettuces or skinning a rabbit, and she had sent Gwen to tell me that she couldn't meet me because she had gone to have six stitches put in her arm, maybe I could have persuaded Gwen to come to the pictures, and back here afterwards. Perhaps she would be a lot less awkward when Alice wasn't around, a different person altogether, in fact, and would even have come with me to the nearest fields or woods. I felt a bit ashamed at thinking this, knowing how impossible it was, but liked to dwell on it while in bed on my own. Gwen would never be that kind of person – I would stake my life on it.

I didn't know why I was stuck in this strange bed-and-breakfast hotel in Stafford but liked being where I was because I was no longer at home. At least I knew something for sure. I couldn't lay still, opened the window to let in air and look at the stars. Night always smelled better than day. A breeze shifted the clouds aside, and showed the buckle of Orion's belt balanced in the sky. Rigel and Betelgeuse were pinpointed. The Dog Star was as bright as ever, and Aldebaran kept guard on the other side as it looked back at the

Pleiades. I drew the thin curtains which reeked of dusty soil, and there was a slit in the left-hand one as if somebody had ripped it with a knife because they couldn't be bothered to pull it open. Or maybe the runners had got stuck.

I dived into the patch of bed which was still warm. The banging of an outside door shook the window-frame, and a gruff voice which seemed to be in my room but was obviously behind the wall shouted that people should make less blinding noise when by God a man who had worked all day was trying to get some kip. Two or three people came into the house and clattered up the stairs. They fell about the landing, and the man in the next room grumbled himself back into sleep. More doors slammed, then the house was quiet, except for snoring from beyond the head of my bed.

I could hardly wait to see whether or not Alice would keep her promise to meet me in town at twelve so that we could go to the Castle. It was a cert though that if she did turn up, Gwen was sure to be with her.

Second Day

I

The curtains kept hardly any daylight out, and I was bursting, so reached under the bed for the pot. When I was halfway through pissing I noticed that a bloke was asleep on the single bed by the door. I felt straightaway under my pillow for the atlas where my pound notes had been put, and found them safe. I was in an honest house, but you never knew. When I got my trousers on I put the notes in my back pocket.

The stranger was lying fully dressed on top of the bedclothes, except that his shoes and socks were off. His shabby blue pinstriped suit was buttoned up, and I could see he had no shirt on underneath. He must have crept in quietly for me not to have heard, but I suppose I was dead after my long day. He was youngish, with curly black hair and a red weatherstained face, lying on his back with both arms hanging over the side. I must have been barmy to think I would have three bedspaces for four-and-sixpence. It's a wonder half a dozen more blokes hadn't piled into the room.

He breathed gently, eyes half-open, a slit of white under both lids. A smell of beer singed the room, mixed with a pong of sweaty feet. I pulled my shirt over my head, got into shoes and socks, donned my coat, packed my saddlebag, and stepped quietly out.

On the landing a beefy grey-haired man, fully dressed but for his bare feet, came from the room next door. He must have been the one trying to saw a footpath through his dreams all night. 'Is MacGuinness awake yet?'

'Who?'

'MacGuinness.' He held a hairbrush, and drew it across his hair, smelling so much of soap and looking so clean he seemed to be made of it. 'Are you the new tea-lad, then?'

I looked at him gone-out.

He held me by the shoulder. 'By Jesus, we could do with you. It's time, an' all. The other left three weeks ago, after he got knocked over, poor boy. Didn't have any wits about him. They've been promising us a new tea-lad ever since, the devils!'

I disentangled myself. 'I'm sorry, mate. I'm not him.'

'No?'

'I'm just passing through.'

'Are you now?' He wouldn't take no for an answer.

'That's right.'

'Oh well, no harm done. You'd better go down and get your breakfast. But is he with us yet – will you tell me that?'

'Is who with us?'

'MacGuinness.'

'He's dead to the world,' I told him.

'Is that so? He always is.'

I left him wondering why MacGuinness wasn't awake, and followed signs saying dining-room which led downstairs and to the back, where I found half a dozen men sitting at a long table. I laughed at having been taken for a mash-lad, which had never happened to me before. Nobody seemed to know what I was on this journey, and maybe that's what I liked about it.

'You get your breakfast from over there,' the man beside me said.

Knives and forks were put for everyone on the plain wooden table, so I left my bag on a chair and went to the hatchway where Joseph, who had collected my four-and-sixpence the day before, slid over a plate of fried egg on toast, four more slices of bread and butter, and a white mug of tea. He made a chalk mark against my name on the wall so that I wouldn't come back for more.

This was an unexpected bonus of a breakfast. Scraps had been the order of the day since leaving Nottingham, and I was ravenous. Eggs were scarce, and I couldn't remember when I last had a real one. Those we got at home went to my father and my younger brother. I sat at the table and gloried in the abundance of grub, to be swilled down by rich sweet tea.

A man set his plate by me on the wood, and the person to put himself opposite was MacGuinness, who had slept in the single bed beside my spacious one. Getting out, I must have woken him up, but even so he still looked as if, having slept with his eyes partly closed, he'd only had the first instalment of a proper night's rest. Perhaps it was this that caused the man beside me to try taking advantage of MacGuinness's dozy aspect, because when he had scoffed his own egg, his fingers reached over to steal away that of MacGuinness.

I watched, and MacGuinness's eyes seemed more closed than when actually sleeping. He was in a trance, as if he couldn't decide whether it wouldn't be better to have a big swig of half the tea in his mug, or a go at his egg on toast to get back to the shock of full-blown day.

On a dresser by the wall, a small green bird was singing its heart out, heard suddenly above the voices of the men. I wondered whether it would still sing if I set it free, but it wasn't mine to tamper with. A man came in and talked to it, drew his nails along the bars before sitting at the table.

There was a crafty look in the eyes of the man whose hand went towards MacGuinness's egg, but the craftiness wasn't steady enough, neither strong nor sure of itself. It was a powerful craftiness, nevertheless. The nearer the hand got to the actual egg the more greed there was in the man's expression, yet it continued wavering from one mood to another. He was fair and thickset, with a pink face that even open-air work hadn't turned almost brown like some of the others. Sensing the coming eruption I tried not to look, in case he should think to blame me for what I thought would be his probable defeat.

I shot up on my seat, because whatever expression the man had, it seemed as if he'd now have shellshock for life. But his overriding cry was one of pain. MacGuinness was another labourer billeted in the house, and sure knew how to look after himself. From the picture of sleepiness, he struck like a snake. His fork came down with great force on the meaty hand about to drag his fried egg off the piece of toast. After the crash, knifing and forking stopped. Mugs rested on the wood, or hung suspended under freshly shaved chins.

The middle fingers of the injured hand, fully outspread, pointed back to the blue mark which was turning rapidly red. If lines had been drawn from them they would certainly have crossed at that point where a cobra with three teeth had done its work. The man looked at his hand as if it had turned into a corpse. 'I was only playing. I was only having a joke, so 'elp me!'

Cheers and laughter went up from the rest of the navvies, but what surprised me as much as the sight of the fork stabbing down was that the injured man didn't draw the mauled hand to safety, but kept it at the scene

71

of the attempted crime – or joke. And MacGuinness who had stabbed him didn't then go on to use his fork for the ordinary purpose of breakfast, but held the weapon over the man's hand as if at any moment he might bring it down again, on the understanding that if the first blow had been to save his egg, the second would be punishment. It was hard to think the danger was over, as long as the man kept his hand there, even though it was crippled. Or perhaps it wasn't yet crippled to the right specifications. I knew that mine would have been. For a long time, at least while his egg and tea got cold, MacGuinness's weapon-hand stayed in position, as if frozen there.

I wanted to see how the contest would end. So did everybody. But there wasn't an end. Maybe the drama happened often, or at least twice weekly. Perhaps it was a game somebody or other was expected to play. I was ready to defend my own egg, though not seriously, and certainly not with the same kind of skill as MacGuinness had shown. Since I wasn't a paid-up member of their society, not even the mash-lad part of it, I assumed I could get on with my breakfast.

The hovering hand that was armed with a fork, and the injured hand at its mercy below, changed positions only slowly. The contest had become so elementary that it was impossible to think of the man with the fork anymore as MacGuinness. He seemed to have been born with it in his hand. Hand and fork were one unit. But the offending hand was also part of the unit.

I didn't know who moved first, or began the retreat. MacGuinness was eating breakfast, and the savaged hand was being nursed under its owner's arm, as if the hand had not been part of him at the time of its misdemeanour, but a wayward pet which had got into a spot of bother out on the table. And though the pet hand should not have acted in such a sly and thieving way, it was loved nevertheless, so that after the uncalled-for stabbing it was being brought back to comfort by this show of tenderness and concern.

A second wave of laughter cracked through the room. A man went out and came back with a tiny bottle of iodine which he poured over the injured hand as if, should it fester, the man might not be able to work tomorrow, a prospect which was beyond the rules of the game. The fiery liquid created ten times more pain than before, for which he got little thanks. The man with the bad hand was treated like a hero, however, and MacGuinness who had brought down the bull's-eye fork was banged on the back out of gratitude at having given everybody such a good show.

The man next to me mopped up the last pond of fat on his plate with a slice of bread. He leaned towards my ear. 'His mother died last month. That's what makes him so sharp. He couldn't even get to the funeral. MacGuinness used to be very easygoing.'

A wireless stood on a dresser by the door, and I tried to make out what the announcer said. He was talking about Labour and Conservative, and I supposed it had something to do with the General Election. One man tried to get a bit of quiet in the room, but nobody took any notice.

II

The gap between two clouds sparkled. Their summits turned fleecy, and light dazzled the window. Joseph, who was the gaffer of the boarding house, unlocked the shed, and I wheeled out my bike to pump up the tyres. He also looked at the sky, as if surprised that the dilapidated house and overgrown garden should look so fresh and sunny. He watched me working the pump.

'Are you after a job?'

I laughed. 'No thanks.'

He knelt, nearer my ear, as if with a secret to tell. 'Where did you come from yesterday?'

I told him.

'Are you running away from home?'

I unscrewed the connection to the back tyre. 'Not likely.'

He moved, to let me get at it. 'We can find you a job on the building site.'

'It'd kill me.' He didn't know I was joking.

'Not a strong lad like you. The men here earn more than ten pounds a week. They're all Irish – or most of 'em are – and they'll look after you. We all stick together. You'll soon get used to the heights. Yes, they're a very good set of lads.'

'I can tell they are.'

He winked. 'Not an IRA man among 'em!'

My arm went in and out twenty times at each tyre, and when I pressed my thumbs on they were as hard as rock. 'I've already got a factory job.'

He wiped the pipe stem against his sleeve. 'You'll lose your roses, working in them places. This work's in the open air. You'll stay healthy.'

Not with a broken neck, I thought. But it was more tempting than he knew. Never go home. No more factory, or Cadets, or aerodrome. They would probably even get me out of joining up. I would work in the Stafford area and see Alice all I liked. On the other hand my life's interest would be gone, and Alice would surely turn her nose up at a building labourer. As for Gwen, if I passed her in the street, she would assassinate me with scorn. 'Thanks, all the same.'

74

He banged me on the back. 'Good luck to you, then,' and walked into the house. I hadn't said more than half a dozen words and they wanted me to be one of them. They were even friendlier than the blokes in the factory. I marvelled at it. No wonder he thought I was barmy not to take him up on his offer. But I knew what I was doing, or thought I did, which seemed to be the same thing.

Two men sitting on the front steps lowered their newspapers and asked where I was going. When I said I didn't know because I was on holiday they called: 'That's the ticket, mate!'

I rode out of town. Going downhill was pleasant because I could sit with one cheek on the saddle, giving the other a rest from the ache which had set in since yesterday. A sore arse was the curse of biking, but it never lasted long.

At the aerodrome an Airspeed Oxford was being wheeled across the road, from the runways into a hangar, while another lifted off from the flat land of the airfield and went low over the lane. I watched others being made ready. Engines sounded in all directions, though there weren't as many planes as last year. The huts where we had stayed at annual camp were in the same place. I whistled a tune from 'The Arcadians' which I'd heard on the boarding house wireless. A magpie was dancing on the road, almost jitterbugging, looking for grit or maybe just enjoying the wind, hopping up and down as if somebody was playing music to a special rhythm it heard but nobody else could.

I rode down the track to Wishdale Abbey. KEEP OUT was painted on a board, so Gwen was partly right, though I think it had always been there. If it had, we hadn't noticed. Bullocks in the field between me and the gardens drifted away, as if they had scented better grass somewhere else. Rhododendron bushes in the distance made a purple patch at the edge of a large wood. I walked through the area of trees and left my bike in a hiding place so that I could go into the ruins. The Abbey wasn't as well-defended, anyhow, as Gwen had hinted. Somebody had already made a gap in the wire, but I rolled a few strands up and made it bigger.

In the main building the charred beams of the roof looked a long way off. It was another world up there, but I was frightened to climb up and explore. Roses in the courtyard didn't smell as good as they had the year before, when there had been lots of rain. Many were dead, but I supposed they might come back to life, or new ones would push out from behind. Large pink petals were like pieces of skin nicotined at the edges, as if to wrap one round a cut finger would cure it. I pissed by a bush hoping it would grow more quickly, though certainly my boot wouldn't, where most of it sprayed.

Bits of tile and sandstone crunched as I went up the steps. If you wanted to do something it was best not to think. I trod slowly, hoping nothing would stop me feeling my way, and wary of the drop to my left showing more and more space between me and the ground.

Doves warbled somewhere above. I didn't look, in case I lost balance, but kept my eyes beaming at the walls, more nervous that some farmer or gamekeeper would catch me at my kid's game of trespassing than of slipping off and breaking an arm and a leg. I seemed too old to be caught, too old to be trespassing. I was a workman of long standing, as well as a flying training candidate who ought to know better. But I couldn't stop climbing.

The stairs felt solid, and I was soon at the first line of rafters. The wood was dark and slippery, but didn't

76

creak much when I used the beams as stepping stones to get across to the staircase leading to the top floor.

Names, mottoes and messages had been scratched on the brickwork with knives or nails, one saying – as one of them always must – KILROY WAS HERE. The stairs had dribbled away at the edges so I spread my palms against the wall as if sweat would glue me there. I had heard it was easier going up than descending, but a vibration underfoot made it seem as if a train was rumbling through a cutting, though the nearest line was miles away. I wanted to slow down for a breather, yet had to go on a few more steps. Then I took them one at a time, treading as if to persuade the stairs that I had no weight at all.

Nothing was written on the wall. If they had got this far they had been in no mood for writing, which was strange, if it was true. I wanted to go back, knew that I should, but my boots kept lifting, step by step, until a row of blackened beams were just above my head, so regularly spaced I was reminded of prison bars. Beyond was the sky, and I dared myself to look. Individual large clouds were spreading across with such purpose that they seemed to have a definite place to go to. I craved to get up there and see where it was, though I might never be able to pinpoint the spot or know about it. I waited to stop trembling and then, telling myself not to be so loony, reached for the nearest beam where the stairs ended, and jumped.

I had only ever been this far from the ground with a parachute under me, and two engines to stop me needing it. I sweated but stayed calm, laughing to myself, thankful that my arms were strong from three years in a factory. Climbing about the beams of Wishdale Abbey I felt like a monkey over the abyss. I could lift myself up, and up some more, then over, and

77

onto my feet, till I stood upright with arms horizontal, and walked the tightrope of the narrow plank to see out of the last half-crumbled window all the way to Stafford and the Trent, and another hazier world beyond that seemed better than the one I looked from. I was on the wrong side to see the farm where Alice lived. To clamber over would be certain death. I would have given my right arm, but not my life, to be perched there with a pair of binoculars.

My penknife chipped the brickwork to make two capital letters. No other initials were in the space around. Then I drew a man's head looking over a wall and wrote underneath: WHAT, NO ROOF? I waved to my family, and workmates, and Uncle Fred (up there, I supposed), as well as to Alice, and to the navvies in Stafford now that I had at least got to the level they normally worked at.

I gave the thumbs up, the clenched fist, the Nottingham goodnight, the pub crawl hello, and the smart salute. I was up on the hill, the peak, on top of human stones with nothing, in this place at least, between me and God. A tractor clattered two fields away. The roar of engines carried on the wind, and an Avro Anson lifted from the airfield and came towards me.

It was better being up here than on the ground, but I would rather have been in an aeroplane at five thousand feet. More was visible from the pilot's canopy than I could see from my dangerous perch. With an aeroplane you were bracketed by a couple of engines, and had wings on either side. You were moving. What land you could see changed slowly all the time. There were bumps underneath, and you might suddenly spiral into the soil and never get back into the light, but any risk was better than being attached to the ground, even if you had climbed as far as you could get above the humid gardens of Wishdale Abbey.

I only hoped I would be able to grab a beam or buttress on my way down. But if I fell there would be no point in caring, no time between the whizz and the bang. If Alice Sands and me were walking with arms linked in that green blur of bushes I'd have thought this the best place to be. Yet I couldn't think so, even though I'd have liked more than anything else in the world to be with her.

I stood a long time between sky and ground, wanting to stay where I was. It seemed unnatural to descend, a waste of the effort of having shinned up. But I was not on my own territory, and that's what trespassing meant. Being so close to the sky, I had to possess what I stood on, then I would deserve to be where I was. Not only that, I'd get hungry if I stayed up here. I might fall. I'd go down like an unexploded bomb. Whoever owned the place, I had got myself into a dead end, and found out that you couldn't travel upwards as easily as on the horizontal. And as for going down there would be no difficulty if you missed your footing. Thinking made me sweat.

There was fear in the soles of my feet and at the back of my spine when I changed position from east to west and back again. One minute I couldn't have cared less, while seeing spires and villages which I fixed on the map, and the next I had to stop myself getting terrified, which was no condition to be in. There was no point resting on this particular perch. If I stayed I would get fed up, even though the view was more than grand. But if ever I saw Albert again I would boast rather than say I was scared. It was marvellous up there, I would tell him. You can't believe it. I saw everything for dozens of miles.

Mostly I decided to get down because there was nowhere else to go. I didn't like the only direction left to me, which was right under my feet. Looking down didn't give me the confidence that I would get to the bottom in one piece. But I scrambled back the way I had come so quickly that when I stood on Mother Earth by the main building I couldn't believe I had been up at all. It seemed the easiest thing I had ever done.

Bushes were spreading, nettles growing tall, brambles clambering everywhere, bay rose a deep pink and black elderberry pushing in between. Soon the Abbey would fall into absolute ruin, covered by a jungle so dense that no one would know the place had ever been there except for a shadowy mark spotted from a high-flying aeroplane.

III

They came into town on their bikes. I thought they would go right by, laughing and talking down Gaol Gate Street, but Alice saw me wave and they stopped by the kerb. I was disappointed that Gwen had come, though not surprised. Three was more than a crowd, and I felt like making a riot, though a trio was obviously what Alice wanted. Both wore frocks for the warm day, and had mackintoshes tied behind their saddles. I had been hoping against hope that I would see her alone.

'Dad says we've got to show you the highlights of Stafford.'

'He sounds a bit of a card, your dad,' I said.

'Oh, he is. He's always making jokes. He said he'd rather we showed you the highlights than the low life. He was serious about that, though.'

I was glad to find her livelier than yesterday, and flattered that her old man had thought about me. 'I wouldn't mind having another look at Wishdale Abbey.'

Gwen tut-tutted with annoyance, as I'd known she would. 'It's fenced off. We told you – didn't I?'

I couldn't tell them I had already been there that morning, and seen that it wasn't. They might ask why I wanted to go again. They could also have wondered what I had been up to. If I mentioned my skywalking they would have thought I was barmy. It was no use hoping they would say I was brave. 'We could still go there. We might get in.'

'A notice says you aren't allowed to.' Gwen pouted. 'They're all over the place.'

I thought Alice was on the verge of giving in, but I was wrong. 'We're off to the Castle,' she said. 'It's historical. You'll like that.'

She was trying flattery. Maybe she was laughing at me. But I had one last try, even though it would spoil my reputation of being interested in history. 'What's the point of going to the Castle? It's only a ruin.'

'How do you know?'

'The map says so.'

She didn't believe me, until I showed her.

'You can see nearly all Staffordshire from the top,' Gwen said. 'It's a lovely view. Even as far as Wales, when there's no mist.'

'I like the Castle.' Alice shivered. 'It's spooky. It used to be haunted. Somebody got poisoned there.'

'What did they eat?' I said. 'Fish and chips?' They laughed, but it was two against one, so I had to agree. I rode off, and as far as the traffic would allow stayed by the side of red-headed, freckled, gorgeous Alice Sands. I stretched out my arm and touched her fingers on the handlebar. Her lips made a smile, but our bikes wobbled and we had to be careful.

Keeping up with each other, we went fast, over the River Sow and along Newport Road. Gwen followed, and I supposed she felt left out, though neither of us were bothered at that moment. We were together at last, but when I touched Alice's hand again she went ahead like a rocket, and Gwen overtook me after a sly build-up of speed from behind.

I felt angry, but kept at my own rate. They stopped, and were laughing at me for following the way on my one-inch map. They called back that I was a slowcoach, then I raced till I was up front and could shout the same to them.

Back in a group, we laughed together because there was nothing to say. Passing a church opposite new houses on the edge of town we went into the entrance to the Castle grounds. We left our bikes behind some trees and walked up a muddy path. A big wood pigeon came swirling down through the jungle, almost flapping itself to pieces. Stones covered with green mould, as if they were pieces of masonry pulled from the Castle, lay on either side of the track. I walked up without knowing why. To visit a castle wasn't my idea of a holiday, but I had to see it, if only because the girls were determined to go there. I supposed I had to see everything that was on offer, so got in front as if I was leading the advance.

At the end of the tree zone the Castle loomed on a high mound with the wind gusting around. A path curved towards a fence which surrounded the walks. Danger notices said that the structure was unsafe, so we couldn't get through and into the building. I was puffed out from the steep climb, but knew I had come up for the view more than anything else, wishing I had a telescope or field glasses on such a clear day. 'That's what I'd like. I'd be able to see the Welsh hills, and bring everything nearer without having to go there.'

The land was coloured all kinds of green, varied by light and dark patches. A great chunk of Staffordshire was laid out on a plate. 'My father's got some,' Alice said, 'but they don't focus very well.'

'What else would you like?' Gwen wanted to know, 'besides binoculars?'

I didn't have to think. 'Three things, that's all. A watch, a fountain pen, and a compass. I can afford to save up for them, but you can't buy them yet.'

'I expect you'll get 'em soon enough, though.'

I couldn't tell whether she was glad about it or not.

'I hope he will,' Alice said.

Now that I had made the wish it didn't seem important. I scribbled some arithmetic on the margin of the map. 'The Castle's 476 feet high, so the horizon's 29 miles away.'

Gwen asked me if I'd heard the news today.

'What was it?'

'Labour won.'

'How do you know it's 29 miles away?' Alice said.

'I learned it in navigation.' You get the square root of the height, and add one third on. I didn't say the last bit, in case they thought I was showing off.

'A castle's got to be high up,' Gwen said, 'to keep everybody out.'

I imagined her boiling the oil, Alice pouring it, while I was trying to get up the wonky ladder, blood pouring from my head. There must be a better way to capture the place than that, I thought. But the old ruin couldn't even keep the rain off you, though it looked intact from the outside. If we walked on it the whole bloody pile of bricks might crumble, like a lot of those historical structures which were so rotten they'd kill you if you got too close and tried to break into them. Unless the gates were opened, and the best studded door pulled ajar, and lights were set glowing in all the windows, and people were beckoning me in to become part of the feasting, I wanted nothing to do with it.

'Look at him,' I heard Gwen say. 'He's miles away. I wonder where he is? I'll bet the place isn't on his map!'

I didn't think it was, but I had to get back to earth for Alice's sake, and also for mine. I only saw a ceiling of cumulus cloud over the dark view, though the sun came through a few gaps in places. An enemy could hide among thickly packed trees below the slope, creep close and maybe take the Castle by surprise. I pictured myself defending the Castle, then leading the attack from below, but didn't know finally where I belonged.

'Dad brought us here for a picnic, last year,' Alice said. 'He had some extra petrol for his car. Then we went on to Rugeley to see Uncle Maurice.' She frowned towards the trees, as if a bogeyman might come out and start chasing her. I held her hand while Gwen went to have a look at the other side of the Castle, as if she had decided she could leave us alone now that she was sure I wouldn't be staying another night in Stafford. I pressed Alice's warm hand, and she looked at me. I asked why she had come to meet me this afternoon.

Her glance turned into a stare. I don't think she saw anything. 'You biked all the way from Nottingham, and we wanted to show you the Castle at least.'

An aeroplane flew low, and when it banked we saw both pilots. Gwen waved at them as she came along the path. I don't suppose they saw her. Maybe she knew them. Twin-engines roared towards Wales.

I liked Alice, yet didn't know why. I was baffled that I didn't know what there was to know about her, in which case how would I remember her when I got back to Nottingham? I couldn't stop thinking about it, yet I had to think about it, because anything you daren't think about you're afraid of. I never thought of dying, on the other hand, yet couldn't care whether I lived or died. But that didn't matter. Only Alice mattered.

All I knew for sure was that I would never be able to find out what it was about her that I liked while with her, and the reason was that she didn't want me to, and I didn't know how to make her want me to, though with somebody else it might have been different, though she wasn't somebody else, but it certainly needed two to be willing to find out things like that.

'It's time I pushed on.' I didn't know why I decided to do something I didn't want to do. 'I'd like to reach Tamworth at least, before dusk.'

'That should be easy,' Gwen said brightly.

We walked down the hill, away from the Castle, and I was never so glad to turn my back on anything in my life. We got on our bikes and rode to Stafford, too separated to talk.

We met again by the bridge, where the road went towards Lichfield. 'I'll see you some other time.'

Her look was halfway between shedding tears, and distaste at me being so close. She tried to smile, and now that we were parting I found it less difficult to know her feelings. I sensed that this was the part of my visit to Stafford she liked most. She had something to come alive at, and could like me because I was responsible for it.

'Will you write to me?'

'As soon as I get home,' I promised. 'Will you write back to me?'

She fiddled with the lamp on her bike, and nodded. 'By the time you get to Nottingham there'll be a letter waiting. I'll do it tonight. After I've had my bath. I like writing letters.'

'It'll be something to look forward to.' I thought she was only promising so that it would be easier for me to leave. She sounded too positive. It was already easy.

'You'll write to me, won't you?'

She seemed to be reading my thoughts. If only she'd done it earlier. 'I will. The minute I get in the house.'

I was convinced she believed me at last, and I didn't like myself for feeling baffled and sick. Gwen, holding their bikes, became sarcastic. 'When will that be?'

She didn't know how much of a help she was. 'In about a week.'

'Do you promise?' Alice wanted to know.

What more could I say? Her breath was close. She looked in the pit of despond, lips bleak and eyes almost closed; and yet I felt she was acting, enjoying her part, and because of that I just wanted to get away from it. So I nodded, and thought that perhaps I would write, after all. But I didn't want to think about it, only to scatter. It was as if I had been living with her all my life.

'Will you send me a photo?' she said.

'All right. Will you send me one of you?'

'I'll put one in my letter. It was only taken a month ago.'

'Thanks.'

All that could be managed was a brief kiss, by me. It was as if I was dying, not going. I kept a straight face.

I watched them ride away in silence, and when I got on my bike I didn't bother to stop and look back. Why I took the south-easterly road to Lichfield and Coventry I'll never know. All I felt was that my road couldn't end in Stafford. It had to go on, until it came back to where I was, in myself.

IV

The fading posters of Captain S. Swingler, the Labour candidate who had won in Stafford, were still pasted to hoardings and walls as I passed through the long street of houses on my way out of town. To go back to Nottingham was the only sensible course, but there was something unfinished I still had to do: to cover more ground, get further away, see other places. I wanted my fill of space. Split for every direction at once, I could have gone north, east, south or west after Alice Sands rode away, as if wild animals were tearing at me. Nothing mattered. The roses of Wishdale Abbey had turned sour. I'd never see her again. She wouldn't even write to me.

I headed south-east and hardly knew why. Each turn of the pedals needed more urgency than I had got, yet I pressed on, into the country, dragging the force from somewhere. I didn't care where I was going, hadn't even looked properly at the map, rode as if something was rotting in my mouth that was impossible to spit out.

I was happy to be on the move. There was no wind, yet I bent almost double to ease a pain in my stomach, going by factories, over a railway bridge and a scummy meandering river, then a canal with painted barges moored to the side. A man fed oats to a horse that had probably hauled him and his cargo, and maybe his family and a cat as well – not to mention a dog – all the way from Worcestershire.

By half past three, after a bit of a climb out of Stafford, I felt I had lived two years since dawn, and would have gone in for a cup of tea to ease my thirst if any place had been open. Sweat dripped from my forehead as I went by Weeping Cross, through Walton, and over the open space of Shugborough Common. I bought a bottle of lemonade and, stopping for a swig while it was still cool, put it back at one go.

Pumped up with wind, I belched my way along, and then got into a spate of hiccups. Traffic was slack, and the birds, made irritable with summer pickings, created a din as if arguing over a dead body in the bushes. The green sleeve of the curving road pulled me forward.

A cotterpin worked loose, causing a delayed action at the pedal before the foot felt the comforting grip as it clicked into place. It was a small gap, but the pedal would drop off unless the cotterpin was hammered in with brute force though not too much ignorance. I didn't want to stop and sort out my tools, hypnotized as I was by the curves and ups and downs, and as tired as if I'd done seventy miles instead of seven.

The tree-lined banks of the narrowing road hemmed me in from the views. Hot and thirsty, my eyes wanted to close, but chagrin kept me going. I faulted myself for not having stayed in Stafford. I could have phoned Alice tomorrow and no doubt seen her again. I didn't know how to use time. I was in too much of a hurry, had no patience, wanted everything to happen at once, on my terms, at my own speed. I had left too quickly. No wonder I never got anywhere. But I had done it, and couldn't turn back. There was never any turning back. Each step forward was fatal, finished. The fickle finger of fate flicked you about like a tiddly-wink. I knew that much, even if I didn't know or care where I was going.

I wanted to get behind a broad straggling hedge and lie down, but I passed all gaps, and pressed on, each foot forward in spite of the loose cotterpin. The hill beyond Longdon was a killer. Any other day it would have been a pimple. You should never regret anything, yet I always did. What happened could not be helped. If it turned out that I had got TB I wouldn't be much bothered, but I supposed that by not caring it would only mean that I didn't have it. It was hard to win when you wanted to.

Place names on the map were familiar, but I didn't know which one I'd end up at that night. The road was restful at the moment, and would go on being so for as long as I only looked at it as if I had never seen it before. I couldn't decide what made me feel so knackered, and knew I would have to stay the night in Lichfield rather than lie down under a hedge. By then I would have done twenty miles, and would not feel ashamed to call it a day.

I hoped to do more tomorrow, but the road after Lichfield did not exist, went over the precipice into the melting-pot. In the meantime, I bore down on the pedals and eased my way along. At one steep hill I got off, plodded, head forward, not knowing what was wrong. The picture was mixed up when I tried to see beyond the edge of the world. I had dropped into an endless cleft of headache and weariness, and sweat on my face turned cold when the wind veered.

I thought of all the houses seen on my first seventy miles, and the ones I might still see. Tens, hundreds, thousands of them. Houses with bow windows neatly bricked and freshly painted, with gleaming roofs and spruce gardens. Houses with white beams and shining slates. Houses with windows shaped like those in churches, with metal latticework and patches of coloured glass. Houses that were lodges, bungalows or inns, every one a gem set in orchard or dell. Houses with long windows of impeccable glass, with polished furniture and books inside, with neat kitchens and cosy parlours, so many comfortable rainproof shelters for any one of which I would have given my soul. At night all the dwellings had lights, and in winter fires glowed from shining black-leaded grates.

For such a dream I resumed my slow advance, wanting every house I saw, even the smallest crumbling residence on the roadside with almost no garden, knowing it would be paradise to get inside and sleep. A far-off cottage at the corner of a wood, with no apparent lane leading that way, had a wisp of smoke at its chimney and a slant of sun on the eaves. I could imagine the smell of stew on a frosty morning, the best of life-giving odours, though at the moment the tang of frost seemed more inviting than the stew.

I wondered if I was going to die. The last time I had been ill was when I was fifteen and got up one morning to go to the factory. I could hardly stand, and knew something was wrong, so set off the half-mile to the doctor's place at Lenton. Not one landmark was registered through the hard frost. All I knew was the effort of moving, and suddenly I was ringing the bell of the house and noticing that the name on the plate was Loewenthal.

'Well, what's wrong with you?' he asked.

'I don't feel well.'

He looked at me for a couple of seconds. 'No, you don't *look* too well, either.'

His tone was a mixture of sternness and unmistakable concern, and struck me as so unusual that I smiled. He was acute enough to know that I wasn't my normal self, and in any case no doctor had ever responded to a statement as to how I felt. My mother said he was a Jew who had to leave Germany because of that swine Hitler, and everybody in the district said how good he was.

With the certificate and prescription in my pocket, I walked home, saying over and over to myself in the doctor's accent: 'No, you don't look too well, either,' and feeling slightly better than when on my way there. He had told me to go to bed but I sat in front of the fire all day, dozing in a chair.

To get to any house meant going on and on, at least as far as Lichfield, where I could pay for a night's bed, because no house on the roadside was mine or, I felt, ever could be. Up the rise of a long hill, clouds were fewer and promised another bout of headache from the metalized blades of the sun. I felt far better than on my visit to the kind Jewish doctor, and knew it for sure when a house I had seen from a distance turned out to be an inn. Even so, no more effort would come out of me, though it was only five o'clock and I hadn't yet reached Lichfield. Wondering what I would have done if there had been no bed-and-breakfast sign on the window, I knocked at the door, feeling as if I hadn't closed my eyes for days, and thinking I could still jerk back into movement if there was no vacant bed.

I dropped my bike against the wall, and hoped whoever was inside wouldn't be long. Yet it was useful that I had to wait, because while standing with the atlas open – in case there was no space and they needed to point out a village where there might be – I got my wind, stopped sweating, and came back into myself.

Three army lorries went towards Stafford, two rows of soldiers inside each. I wanted to be one of them rather than where I was. They were going to camp to have their tea, which would be followed by a stint in the NAAFI before going to bed. But space in a cool pub would be better, and I wondered why the landlord or his wife were too dead to answer. My second knock was on its way when a slapped bolt sounded against wood and a woman wearing a flowered apron asked what I wanted.

She had grey hair, and weighed me up through wire glasses that, with the cast in her left eye, put something gentle and questioning into her gaze. She was a careful woman who looked after herself well, though it hadn't always been easy. Whenever she failed to do something properly it was only because she could do nothing about it. Her father was a coalminer, and her grandfather had been a farm labourer. I would have figured out more about her, but my body and soul together spoke the question: 'Have you got bed-and-breakfast here for tonight?'

'There is,' she said, 'but it's dormit'ry.'

'Dormitory?'

'Twenty beds in a big room. Lorry drivers stay here, as well as cyclists, though I don't know's there'll be many of 'em in tonight.'

I would have taken a barn or a potting shed. Even a tent wouldn't have come amiss. I laughed to myself. 'I don't mind at all.'

'Come on, then, and I'll show you.'

I was happy following her through the bar, behind the counter and into her kitchen where a clock ticked against the wall. A big fire, in spite of the close day, burned in the grate, and as we walked by a few more crannies and corners I waited for us to branch off and ascend to a room upstairs.

But she led me into the garden, where the crimson skins of tomatoes pressed against the inside glass of a greenhouse. Around the back door were white roses, marguerites and gilly flowers. There were marrows so big you'd have to carry one under each arm, and cucumbers like the limbs of the Green Man himself.

A ginger cat cleaned itself by the waterbutt, whiskers

springing back from scouring paws. It wore a blue collar but was as thin as a rake, though I supposed it had plenty to eat in such a place. Maybe it had worms, and needed a Bob Martin's. At the far end of the garden stood a long hut on stilts, like a barrack I'd often been glad to sleep in at annual camp.

'That's where you can be.'

It was clean and airy. Windows let plenty of light on two rows of beds, each covered by a thick white counterpane.

'Which one's mine?'

She smiled. 'Any you like.'

I had a choice, but couldn't decide which one I would drop into. 'It looks smashing.'

'We had it done before the war, and I'm glad we did. We've earned a bob or two, though I don't think it's paid for itself yet.'

The score of pallid oblongs confounded me, each with a large white pot underneath, yet I felt lucky at being safe from the road, and the head-aching sun that had made me feel sick.

'Shall you be wanting something to eat?'

I had no appetite, but breakfast had been my last intake, and I knew I ought to have a meal for the evening. 'I wouldn't mind a bite.'

'I'll get it ready, then.'

I dropped my atlas on a bed at the end of the left-hand row, then went to bring my bike into the garden. There was a cooler breeze and more overcast, but a glance both ways convinced me I was best off the road. I fiddled with the cotterpin, but put off mending it till morning.

Cool water in the sink at the end of the room was a blessing, but when I dried myself my face was hotter than before. I moved slowly after getting dressed in case

I was sick, but put on a clean shirt, and rubbed the other with soap at the sink because it stank of sweat. Rinsing it a few times, I pulled at the sleeves and collar to get the worst creases out, then hung it to dry, pushing the clothes-line high with the prop so that it would catch the breeze.

The landlady lifted the hinged part of the bar, and I went through to a small table she had set. I had never eaten at a table on my own before. I wondered where her husband was. Maybe he wasn't much of a landlord, and slept all day. Perhaps he had done a bunk to Canada, gone on the last boat before the war. Maybe he went out to work and was cycling his way back from a factory, cursing every yard, and hankering for his tea. Maybe he was in the Pioneer Corps. Maybe he was dead.

There was a wedge of pork pie, a dish of lettuce and tomato, some bread and butter, and a large pot of tea. She pulled the chair out for me to sit down. I noticed for the first time that half her teeth were missing. She expected me to go at it like a wolf. 'This'll make you feel better.'

'It will. Thanks a lot.'

'Where did you come from?'

'Nottingham.'

'All that way? Well, I never!'

She went off to do her work, thinking I had biked all of it today. Or maybe she'd go off and read the newspaper. She looked as if she would be interested in the news. I drank two cups of tea, then felt ready to eat, thinking maybe I would walk into Lichfield afterwards and look at the town. I should have cycled further, because a few hours of daylight were still left.

'Are you bed-and-breakfasting?'

A girl with sharp face and long blonde hair, which I

wasn't sure was natural, leaned on the bar between the pumps and the till. I twitched with surprise, hoping she hadn't noticed.

'Everybody gets on the move except me,' she said. 'It won't be for much longer, though.'

She wore a red jersey, and took a cigarette from a glittering handbag. Anybody could see I was lodging here for the night. The pub hadn't yet opened its doors for the evening, so I said: 'Do you live here, then?'

She pulled a monkey-face. 'Yes. Worse luck.'

I didn't see much wrong with having a pub as your home. Plenty of work, but you got free booze. And if your parents owned it, you weren't badly off. 'It must be all right.'

'So what?' She almost spat the words out.

I ate a bit. She had a lovely figure. 'What's your name?'

'Eunice.'

'Mine's Paul.' The bread and lettuce was good, but the first mouthful of pie wasn't easy to get down. I didn't want to be sick in front of such a smashing girl, so I went back to the tea, and drained the pot.

'You was dry,' she said, as if I didn't know.

'Why don't you like it here?' There were things I would never understand. Or I would, but if I pretended I wouldn't maybe I'd learn about something I didn't know existed.

She sat down on a form under the window. 'Would you?'

This was a funny how-do-you-do. I said I didn't know.

'Well, I'm asking you.' She almost shouted, as if about to come over and have a go at throttling me.

I knew her sort. There were plenty in Nottingham, whose bark was worse than their bite. 'I suppose so.'

'You wouldn't if you'd got to, like I have.'

'How old are you?' I wanted to know.

'Seventeen. And sometimes I feel seventy.' She looked around the room. 'I've had my bellyful of this lot.'

'I'm seventeen,' I said, hoping she'd like me because it gave us something in common.

'What's that got to do with me?'

'You won't leave your mam and dad, though, will you?' I hoped she wouldn't, and I wanted to tell her not to, but if she didn't take my advice, I wouldn't be able to see her do a bunk.

'Well,' she said, 'you never know, do you? And she's my grandma. My mam died, and my dad hopped it five years ago. I hope the Germans killed him. Somebody ought to. I think so, anyway. And don't you say a bloody word!'

I laughed, wondering whether she wasn't off her head. 'Trust me!'

She puffed her cigarette. 'Who do you think cleans the place up, then? And meks twenty beds every morning? And swabs the bar out with a bucket of soapy water and a rag? And empties all them piss pots?'

Somebody's got to, but she would only have one pot to tip out tomorrow, by the look of it. 'Do you go to work, as well?'

'Don't be so bloody daft. I'm not a machine, am I?' Then she smiled. 'You don't look daft, though.'

'Thanks.'

'Not to me, anyway.'

I couldn't even finish the bread and butter. 'I never thought I was.'

'No, men don't, do they?' She stood close, and looked at me. I looked back. She had a small mole by the side of her nose, and I felt like scraping it off to see whether it was good to eat. But if I did, she might bleed to death, and then I would be in trouble. A terrible attack was made by a vampire on a young woman near Lichfield, the newspapers would say. No clues yet, but the police are closing in. They'd never get me, because I'd go through the cordon on my bicycle, and they'd blame it on somebody who had a car. And fifty years later I'd stand in the rain in Lichfield market-place without a hat on to do penance for my crime.

Her lipstick was smudged. She dropped the smouldering fag-end in my saucer, then stared out of the window as if even blank space was more interesting than me. 'I don't see why men should think they're daft,' I said, 'anymore than women.'

She gave one final look as if to scorch me to the roots, and walked out, her heels clip-clopping across the floor.

I was grateful that she'd kept me awake, but I now felt so dozy it was difficult to stop my head dropping onto the table. Wanting something to read while finishing the meal I went to get my book of wild flowers from the dormitory, and my atlas so that I could plan tomorrow's run. I stood by the greenhouse not knowing what to do, but savouring the smell of garden blooms. The sky was cloudless. With a pang I realized the loss of my guide book, because I couldn't read about all the interesting places I would be going through.

The hut was still empty. I picked up the books but, without thinking, took off my jacket and shoes, pulled down the counterpane, and lay with them in my hand. I was glad I hadn't eaten much. I pedalled. Burning coals melted the tyres as I went along the road. An Airspeed Oxford flew me above the fields clutched in its unretracted wheels. I felt no fear at hanging over such enormous space, the whole of Staffordshire under my waving feet.

97

Alice and me were lying between two large bushes of overblown roses in Wishdale Abbey. They were dripping wet, but we weren't even damp. I couldn't get myself into her, no matter how we moved. Her knickers were in the way, and then her cunt had no hairs round it, and I almost came, but then I heard shouts of anguish, as between my parents when they quarrelled at the worst of times before Uncle Fred went into the asylum, when I was too little to tell what was going on, and I would do a panic-run to hide in the dark under the stairs till it was calm again or my mother fetched me out.

Though in a dream, there was a terrible bout of noise, as if whoever fought would soon stop and then turn to destroy each other. I ran across a wasteground, to bury myself in a field of tall wheat but, no matter how much I burrowed, the shouting followed. I listened, disheartened for a while, then creased with despair. Bitter shouts of murder and mayhem came from inside the pub.

Opening my eyes from sleep, it was dark. A tall bulky man switched on an end light to undress by the door. Wearing only combinations, he pulled back the bedclothes and got in. An enormous mass of people were singing 'Auld Lang Syne' in the distance. He sighed, belched, swore, yawned, and farted. Three hours must have gone by, and I stood up to go out for a walk. Too groggy, I got undressed, and pissed so much into the pot I almost filled it.

Thousands of light crystals blinded me from the window pane, no pattern obvious. I remembered looking up when first being taught to pick out the constellations, how it had been impossible to find my way through so much glittering dust. And then I thought the stars were really dust, of which the earth was also a speck, and that in a cloud of dust shaken from a rag were scores of worlds like the one I was on, with billions of beings called people on each of them, and every person shaking more dust out of a rag, and billions of worlds on each of their specks of dust. I refocused my eyes with an effort that made me dizzy, and for the first time recognized Ursa Major, bright and clear, which seemed to bring everything in the universe to order, or at least enough for me to stand secure on my own feet.

With flashes continually before my eyes, I slipped between the sheets and got back into a land of no dreams, in spite of the other man's snoring. There was no more quarrelling. The doors of the pub were locked, and people had gone to sleep. A dog barked, set off by a jangle of trucks from the railway. The tunnel of sleep was a long one, with many curves. A midsummer cat howled, and I woke to see the door opening, and someone else, Eunice I thought, getting into the man's bed. There were shadows, and a drifting light pulled a shutter of final darkness behind it, hiding her whiter face.

Third Day

I

The spreading tops of potatoes on either side of the path
gave off a smell of rootiness and soil. A cabbage-white
butterfly shivered between the leaves and couldn't make
up its mind where to settle. Catching sight of a tall
green barrier of kidney beans, it struggled up to the top
like an autogyro and disappeared behind.

A smell of frying bacon came from the pub.
Headache and fever had gone as I pumped up my bike
tyres. On a shelf in the shed was, among other tools, a
short-handled hammer, which I borrowed to bang in
the cotterpin. The echoes seemed to shatter the peace
but nobody minded. I gave the chain sprocket a few
drops of oil, and pressed a pedal to circulate it. A cock
opened its crowing gullet. It looked at me as if saying:
'I'll bet you can't do that' – and crowed again. The
wheel spun, straight as a die, and ready for the road.

I folded the clean shirt so that at least the collar
wasn't creased, and put it into my bag. Remembering
Eunice, I got the pot from under the bed and, holding it
so that nobody would see, created a swamp between the
cabbage rows. The sun would take away the stink. To
leave it would have made me a marked man to her
dying day. No one had been in the end bed when I
woke up, though the clothes were so rumpled that I
thought a cyclone had passed that way. I wondered if
he had broken her in. At the sink I swirled a flannel rag
around the inside of the pot, then slid it under the bed
where it belonged.

At the same table as last night the landlady laid out a breakfast of bacon and fried potatoes. There were hunks of bread, and the same brown pot brimming with tea. I enjoyed stuffing myself. Even a fly buzzing around didn't get a look-in. Outside, on the front, the man who had slept in the dormitory hit the large corrugated tyres of his lorry with an iron bar as if defying them to burst, then pulled himself into the high cab like Tarzan, and played with the lighting system. He leapt down again and stood scratching his head, maybe speculating as to whether he should take the lorry to the nearest cliff and push it into the water because it had once tried to nudge him over, and from that time they hadn't got on very well together.

I dropped some rind, and the cat tackled it like a tiger attacking a snake. The end got caught under its collar, and they rolled over and over on the dusty floor. The clock on the wall said a quarter past eight, so I'd slept twelve hours. The hostel map showed a place near Daventry, about fifty miles south-east, and I thought maybe I couldn't help but get there by evening, even taking it easy. I'd be a lot further from Nottingham, and no place was too far. I felt better than ever this morning, and knew it was too early in the week to head in any direction for home.

Eunice thought I was about to say good morning (though I wasn't) and put a finger to her lips to keep me silent. She glowered, prevented the drawer of the till from making a noise as it came out, and shuffled both hands in like an expert. It was nothing to do with me. The drawer slid back. Maybe she did it every day, and her grandparents knew. Stuffing the money in her coat pocket, she blew a kiss, and went out waving goodbye. Noticing her sharp and shapely little nose I thought I had known her all my life, and waved back. She was like a sister I might have had but didn't and was glad I hadn't.

I still wasn't all there after yesterday's fever, and too much nightfall underground. I watched her as if sitting at the pictures, not much connected to it, but I tried to decide what Eunice was up to (if that was her name), and felt sorry for the grandmother at having such a snipe-nosed vixen in the house. Then I got worried, in case somebody thought I had dipped a hand in the money box. I had never stolen anything in my life, and knew that quick wits were necessary if I was to avoid detection, arrest, trial, and a long term of hard labour on the treadmill that would solve all my problems, though not in the way I wanted. Then I remembered that I didn't have any problems.

I still had to escape, come what may, because I wouldn't stand a chance if I stayed to brazen it out. I ought to flee this second, leaving my atlas with the Coventry route marked in black pencil, whereas I wouldn't go that way at all, but head straight into Birmingham, so that the police would never find me. Beyond that maze I would travel by lanes and tow paths, and over fields if they were dry enough, and across page 109 till I reached a vast and undulating forest where I could hide for a while.

I picked up the cat and saw by its collar that the name was Sandy, which matched the colour but not the nature of Alexander. I gave it a piece of fried potato, but the cool nose turned up at a crumb of bread. Wind blew curtains in at the open window, and Eunice was getting into the cab of the lorry. She slipped and banged her knee because the step was high, and her lips made definite shapes of bad language, but a muscle-bound arm pulled her up like a yo-yo. I expected her knee was bleeding. She swore again, and then the door slammed for the whole world to hear. Maybe he was giving her a lift to work, or he would let her down in Lichfield so that she could do the day's shopping for her grandma.

'Do you want some tea, duck?' the landlady said. Her eyes were red, and I supposed she had been crying. It was hard to know whether I ought to betray Eunice or not, but I thought I shouldn't. I turned from the window to get my atlas, and nearly trampled on the cat. It was time for me to go, I told her, and followed her into the parlour.

'That'll be five shillings then,' she said.

The sound of the lorry driving off didn't seem to bother her. It was too late, anyway. She would run down the road and fall in the mud, crying for Eunice to come back, the poor woman too upset to notice her broken glasses. Please God, don't let it happen. The road was bone dry. I felt like crying. Feckless Eunice was off with her fancy man. Half the week's takings were in her pocket, and she would never come back. I bled inside, and the woman thought my tormented expression was because of the long road ahead. Perhaps it was good riddance, and cheap at the price, once she'd got over the shock. Better late than never. I didn't know what to hope for.

The woman sighed, and put the two half crowns into her purse, and as I went for my bike I heard her calling Eunice to come and clear the table of the breakfast pots. I wheeled the bike to the road, trying not to seem in a hurry, but praying for a Frank Whittle jet engine to get me away quickly. Maybe she had told Eunice to go shopping, but thought she hadn't left yet. She was only sighing for something her husband had said. Or perhaps she'd forgotten telling her to go.

I hoped so, but if I wanted to know for sure I had to make up my mind as to what had happened, and decide if it was the truth. Otherwise I would never be much the wiser. The road was clear into Lichfield, but I didn't care to see where Dr Johnson was born. I would go straight through.

II

All the horizons of Warwickshire were different, yet more or less the same. I gloated on how many horizons there were in the world. The more the better, certainly more than I could spot from the high saddle of a bicycle, though they kept me going for the moment. The wide horizon seen on looking back was always less wide than the one in front, and soon forgotten when I stood on my pedals and sent a jet-propelled fart so as to get sooner out of their way.

I hugged built-up areas, and went through Sutton Coldfield, but was careful to turn away from the Birmingham entanglement, following my south-south-easterly route via Castle Bromwich and Bacon's End, by Little Packington and Meriden. Crossing the intricacies of page 128, I wrote details of my track made good on the back of the Stafford one-inch map whose margin I had wheeled myself off yesterday.

I had never been alone for so long. The third day had broken the rope with home and let me freewheel solo into the never-ending green, sheep to one side and cattle on the other. One field was a brown patch, almost orange, with a farmhouse at the edge that I no longer craved refuge in because the tarmac roadway had its own magnetic pull to get me forward. I didn't want to let go of the road, having achieved the breakthrough which a long-distance biker at the factory called Denis

France told me always came on the third day, when legs no longer ached, arse was no longer sore, and breath no longer short.

A memory which puzzled me was of going by bus on a school picnic, to a field somewhere near Burton Joyce when I was five or six. I hadn't seen one like it since. The field was on a corner where a lane joined the main road. I hadn't bothered to look for it since because it had no other distinguishing marks which would tell me which one it was. Only the mystery of rich grass lingered, and as I rode through the area of endless Warwickshire fields I wondered how many had a special place in the minds of people now grown up.

Temporary huts and buildings in the middle of Coventry made the place slummy and crowded. I wanted to get out quick, but spotting a British Restaurant I went in to eat a dinner for a shilling. The place reeked a mile off. As a kid I used to wonder how much nourishment there was in a food smell, and how long you would have to stand in it to feel less hungry. A smell of fat, or fish and chips, seemed so solid that I couldn't believe you wouldn't benefit from it. The smell in an RAF airmen's mess, when I went to cadet camp, was a combination of bacon-and-fried-bread, and the vat of washing-up water in which you cleaned your eating irons afterwards. But a British Restaurant smelled of floorcloths and fatty mincemeat, though even so, at either place, my mouth watered for food before I got through the door, and I was never long enough in the queue for the smell to blunt my hunger.

On the tray I put gravy-soup, a plate of cottage-pie, spuds and butter beans, a section of bread pudding with custard on top, and a cup of coffee. Before me in the line was a woman with grey hair so sparse I could see pink flesh between the roots. Her coat was made of old blanket material, clumsily tailored from purple and brown squares tied together with a piece of rope. In one hand she had a carrier-bag full of something or other, as well as a black handbag, and with the other hand she slid her tray along, loading as she went. She was old enough to have lost her husband in the Great War, and after that she took to the road. Or maybe she had walked out on him when he gave her too many black eyes and cut lips. She had been in Coventry on the night of the blitz, and lost some of her wits but none of her appetite.

The tables were crowded with factory workers, like the place I went to in my dinner hour at home, which was the only thing wrong with it. When someone left I took his space and sat opposite a man with the *Daily Mirror*, seeing the headlines of Labour's big win between one mouthful and the next.

Before leaving town I bought a loaf and a tin of sardines, as well as some apples, reserve supplies which I stuffed in my bag. Trees stippled with sunlight slopped shadows under my wheels. Travelling without object, I had no girl to meet or pal to call for. I sweated and pressed my feet down, pedalling along a road bordered by bushy summer hedges. Out of lush pastures came a real roller-coaster of blue-black macadam, the landscape opening towards high land around Rugby and Daventry.

Coppices of tall aerials on the horizon were as if built with Meccano sets and knitted together with power-lines. I wondered who their transmitters were in touch with. Messages in morse and voice seemed to come humming through the sky, communicating to places in every part of the British Empire.

I leaned on a gate to eat chocolate bought with the last of my sweet coupons. The wireless signals sparking out of the aerials didn't recognize horizons. They found a way over by spinning to the sky and bouncing back, or following the curvature of the earth. I wanted to follow where they stabbed. Signals sprinkled onto strange and wonderful places where the map was coloured red, radiating to ships, bases, barracks and planes, to lonely jungles and desert coastlines, Polar stations and commanding mountain-tops, cities whose boulevards were lined with palm trees, steamers on rivers a thousand miles from the sea.

I didn't seem to belong where my feet were planted. I loved England, but something about it had always stopped me from liking it. I was here only because I couldn't yet be anywhere else. On the other hand, to be locked in moving clockwork on a spreading net of roads in a country I had been born in but couldn't wait to get out of was far from torment, because on the third day of freedom I felt as if I had been on the tramp since birth.

I cycled across page 112. Thick cloud had gaps that shot sunlight onto the straight road. At a glance, all pages of the atlas looked more or less the same: a pale base scored by scratchmarks of railways, the red veins of roads and the grey porridge flecks of towns and cities. Yet all were different when looked at closely, each feature unique when the book was shut and I took in the varying landscape as I rode along.

My brakes squeaked at every steep hill, the black rubber blocks at the wrong angle, so I stopped to adjust them. With forty miles behind me since morning, I didn't feel tired. Perhaps power from the aerials transmitted some energy to me. I wondered whether people who lived around them got the same boost. Their emanations reached Lichfield, and caused Eunice to get into the lorry and abscond from home. I hoped she would be all right, though she had brought off her escape the hardest way, as far as I could see. But everyone had their own method, and mine of having enlisted might not turn out much better, at least to someone like Gwen.

Daventry, Rugby and Droitwich were names I had always noticed on the face of the wireless at home, places whose aerials pumped out the singing of Peter Dawson and the music of the Black Dyke Mills Band. Near the end of the war in Europe the wireless told of a victory every other day, giving news of what was happening on the far side of the world almost as soon as it had taken place. For nearly six years we'd got the good as well as the bad, true as well as false, though we had believed most of it, which in the end made everything true enough. Only the Japanese were still fighting, and it seemed as if they would hold out till doomsday, which would give me a chance to have a go. I wasn't sure now how much I wanted to, but I had volunteered and, being on a conveyor belt, had no option.

While I looked over the bridge of the Oxford Canal, at a red, purple and yellow barge, three other cyclists set their bikes against the parapet. 'That's a beauty,' I heard someone say. 'Look at that paintwork along the side.'

The head of the long barge was passing by a wharf and I thought it would never stop coming out of the cavern of the bridge, as if the gloom of the road tunnel was a workshop manufacturing barges, and the cutter-off bloke had forgotten to do his work when it got to the required length. 'It's sixty foot long, if it's an inch,' another voice said, 'and that's a fact.'

'It's like a bloody pencil.'

Before looking up I wondered who they were, feeling distrust and fear in case they should try to nick my bike

108

or otherwise make trouble. But I was on a freewheeling ride, not in a pub on Saturday night, or in the street outside on my way home. And their quiet and wondrous comparisons struck similarities with my own. 'A stick o' rock, more like,' the first voice said.

'Longer than Churchill's cigar, though I don't suppose he'll smoke 'em anymore.' The barge had a folded pram tied to its superstructure, a man at the tiller naked from the waist up guiding it effortlessly, to the cry of a baby from the cabin.

'He can't tek the kid a walk to stop its gallop,' said the third cyclist. 'It's a bloody noise, though, when everything else is so quiet.'

'He can tek it for a swim.' I looked up and faced them. 'Turn it into a tadpole, maybe.'

The one who had compared it to Churchill's cigar was tall and had spots on his face. He stood astride a bike with no crossbar. 'It wouldn't teach it to find its way around Sheffield, either,' he said. 'I suppose them barge kids are lost in town streets.'

'You'd be lost on water, wouldn't you?'

'I expect I would. But not in Sheffield, and that's all as counts.' He took a bottle of water from his saddlebag and drank it dry.

It was obvious where they came from. I asked where they were going. The one who had said it would be hard to take the baby for a walk to stop it crying told me they were heading for the youth hostel at Crawby. I said I was, as well.

'Did you book in advance?' Sheffield asked.

I hadn't.

Neither have we. Let's hope we get there early enough to find some beds vacant. We left Sheffield yesterday morning, and slept last night in a field near Ashby-de-la-Zouch. My bones still ache, it was that damp.'

'We'll have to do the same again if the hostel's full,' said the one who had been most impressed by the colours of the barge. 'My name's Pete Clipstone.'

'We've been getting lost all day.' Sheffield accused everyone for their bad luck, even me. 'Zigzagging here there and everywhere. I suppose we'll get to Crawby about the middle of next week.'

'I could do with a wash, so I'd like to get there sooner,' Pete said.

I told them they could follow me if they liked, though I hoped they wouldn't want to, because I could then get to the hostel first and have a better chance of finding a bed.

'You're just the bloke we need.' Noah saw my atlas. 'Our map's too small-scale. It only shows continents.'

'Crawby's not much more than ten miles off,' I said. 'You keep on to Daventry, and go two miles out by the Banbury road. We'll soon know whether they've got any beds.' They thought I'd been there every year for the last five. But I hadn't. I'd been almost nowhere. Sheffield said they hadn't, either, except in England, though that was more than good enough for them. They fetched biscuits and lemonade out of their packs. I had toffees, and we stoked up.

Sheffield had a woman's bike, while the other two – Pete and Noah – mounted a tandem. The four of us set off. They lived on the same street, and worked in the same factory. Sheffield was an apprentice in the engineering shop, and Noah, who plied the front handlebars of the tandem, was an electrician's apprentice. Pete worked in the stores department.

'We've been promising ourselves a nice long spin since Christmas,' Sheffield said.

They wondered why I was on my own. So did I. And

I wouldn't have been if Albert hadn't let me down. But I wasn't bothered about that anymore. 'I couldn't get anybody to come with me. My mate thought it was too far.'

'Bloody 'ell!' they said, and therefore seemed the right friends for me.

The steep hill got steeper beyond Barby village. 'Make way for the road-eaters!' Sheffield shouted to a couple of snotty-nosed kids who stood by the palings of a cottage garden.

We laughed till we were puffed out. I wobbled up front, the tandem in the middle, and Sheffield coming behind on a grid that rattled even more than anybody's. All our bikes made some sort of noise. Going in spurts, racing and falling back, then catching up again and wheeling in front, each hill seemed shorter, though Sheffield turned so purple that his spots nearly disappeared.

We were on a six-hundred-foot ridge the whole way to Daventry. Rivers spread in all directions through England, according to the coloured map with the youth hostel handbook. 'We can tell the blokes at work that we went to the middle of the country,' said Sheffield, 'when they ask.'

'They'll be too much in the middle of next week to bother,' Pete told him.

'Who wouldn't – at Blackpool?'

We stood at the Kilsby-Willoughby crossroads to get our wind back. 'They'll ask, though,' said Noah. 'It's as sure as Ohm's Law. We allus have a natter in our dinner hour.'

I asked what Ohm's Law was. Did they hang you if you broke it? Or did you only get fined? I saw Noah's broad face and gingerish hair, when he looked up from the road, as he had probably been at the age of ten, one of those kids who stood at street corners with a penny tablet of paper and a stick of pencil writing down car numbers. He spelled it out for my benefit: 'It's when the current in a conductor is directly proportional to the applied voltage.'

'You can tell he goes to night school,' said Pete. 'He's always blinding us with science. But he only goes there so's he can get off with the girls.'

'I'll be on OHMS Law next year,' I told them, hoping they'd see it, 'when I get my papers.'

'We're in reserved occupations,' said Sheffield, 'being apprentices. No bloody army for us.'

'Nor navy, either.' Noah spat, but not much came out. 'I'd rather be a Bevin Boy.'

'Bevin's a bastard,' Pete swore, 'making lads go down the pit when they don't want to.' Locks of dark curly hair hung over his forehead, the palest face of us all. The combination of brown eyes, and a firm mouth with lantern chin, made it look as if the top part of his head had been stuck at random on the bottom. 'My mate's brother had to go down the pit, and now he's crippled for life. He was all set for a Brylcreem Boy till Bevin got hold of him. Anybody mentions Bevin in that house and they get thumped.'

Sheffield poked me as I went by. 'That leaves you and Pete to finish the war for us. Pete's only in the stores, aren't you, duck?'

The wind made us lark about like kids of four, a release after the low land, and the clutter of Rugby aerials. I led the way. Maybe such blips played hell with our tripes. We felt good though, nothing but joshing, so that in no time we were sailing past a reservoir and down into Daventry, through the gates and along the High Street without stopping. I was in front and couldn't get at the atlas to check our way, me and Sheffield making the tune of the Light Cavalry Overture so loudly that people shopping looked as if we'd gone daft. We veered right at the second turn where the climb began again, while Pete and Noah on the tandem shot straight on. Half-way up the hill, we almost pissed ourselves laughing when they came back spitting tacks at their mistake.

III

The thin, sandy-haired warden with pale grey eyes sat pondering on the registration book as if the laws of the world were written there. 'Yes,' he said, trying to bite his moustache, 'some beds are still free.' After a final nod he took our shillings and membership cards, then inscribed names and addresses as if we were going to stay at the place forever.

The hostel was two long houses made into one, situated at the main-road end of the village. Under the thatched roof were blocks of bunks. A couple of dozen bikes and another tandem leaned against the stone wall. The single tricycle was allowed to stand on the grass. The gate latch clattered with continual coming and going. We were lucky to get in for the night.

A man with a handkerchief on his bald head was showing off before the girls by jumping over the wooden fence. The warden saw him from the office, and shouted that if he didn't behave he would be out on his neck: 'A silly fool did that last year, and broke his ankle.'

'Sorry, warden.' The man winked at us, and waved towards the windows of the women's dormitory across the street. The warden shook his head, half-smiling as he walked away. When he came back Noah asked if somebody called Jack Randall had stayed there last night. 'We're supposed to meet up with him.'

The warden flipped the pages of his book. 'He did. I remember him. He practically cleaned the whole place before he left. Even offered to weed the vegetable garden. A good chap, that one.'

'He's from Sheffield,' Noah said. 'That's why.'

'It says here that he came from Doncaster,' the warden snapped, though I thought I saw him wink at himself.

'Just like old Jack to tell a fib,' said Pete.

'He spoils it,' Noah said. 'He'd do owt for a lark.'

'Who is he?'

'Only a pal,' they told me.

'You'll get your cards back in the morning,' the warden said, 'if you've done the sweeping and washing to my liking.'

Upstairs, I bagged the bottom bunk, and Pete shinned to the top one. Sheffield slung his belongings on the next bed along, while Noah claimed the one over that. Stripped to the waist we queued in the ablutions, painted ourselves with soap suds and then pressed fingers at the tap to squirt each other clean, keeping watch for the warden.

'I wonder how he lost his arm?' Noah said.

Pete buttoned his shirt. 'Got run over by a bus, I expect, coming out of a boozer at Saturday dinner time.'

'I'll bet he don't drink,' Noah said.

We clattered down the narrow stairs in single file.

'Why don't you ask him to his face?' Sheffield said.

On our way back from hanging the towels to dry we saw the warden slotting a sheet of blotting paper into his membership book.

'Ask him,' Noah said.

'I'm boggered if I will.'

I stood back, but not so far that I couldn't listen.

114

'You're bloody frightened,' said Sheffield.

'You ask him, then.'

He turned on Noah. 'Who, me?'

'Yes, you. Go on.'

'Now then,' said the warden, 'what's all this arguing about? I can't have that kind of shouting on my premises. You're on holiday. You're supposed to be all pals together, aren't you?'

Turning a bloodier red than I had so far seen, Sheffield blurted: 'How did you lose your arm, sir, if you don't mind telling us?'

Irritation on the warden's face changed to a sly smile, and he looked as if wondering whether he should advise us not to waste his time. 'I caught it in a mangle.'

'A mangle, sir?'

He smiled. 'A Jerry one. Now let me get on with my work. It takes twice as long with one arm!'

They laughed, praising Sheffield for his audacity, and thumping him when he grinned as if he deserved it. We queued in the kitchen to get a stove, and I toasted thick slices of my loaf, sharing the sardines with the others, who put in boiled spuds and slivers of cheese. Pete had packets of tea and a tin of sugar from the stores he worked in, so we drank a strong brew till spots played leapfrog before our eyes. Sheffield suggested we go to the pub and water it down with pints of ale.

I felt fresh enough to do another stint on the bike, though I was glad the day wouldn't live much longer. Crawby, in the valley of the Nene, was sheltered from the wind. We stood in what was left of the sun so as to stay warm as long as possible. Pete and Noah, weather flushed, rolled up their sleeves for it. Even Sheffield, no longer agonized by grinding hills, looked healthier and less blemished.

I'd hardly thought of Alice Sands all day, but her vivid face came to me as I leaned against the pub wall and tried to picture whether she was at home helping to cook supper, or out in Stafford with Gwen and a couple of youths. A shaft of misery went through me because I wanted to be with her, but I knew I had let every opportunity slip beyond reach. If I set off early in the morning I would easily get back to Stafford by evening, but it would be like swimming against the Mississippi current. I would arrive in time to telephone, and ask her to come out with me.

'Sorry, I can't,' she would say.

And I would ask: 'What about tomorrow, then?'

And she would say: 'Well, what about it?'

'I'm asking you,' I would say.

Her silence at this question put me off. My imagination went blank. You couldn't predict the future without evidence. I was fixed on a course never to see her again, unless I hot-pedalled it to Stafford in the morning. And then I would know for sure. But how much for-sure did I really want to know? I'd have to wait till I got home and found her letter.

'Drink up,' Sheffield said. 'The publican's crying out for trade!'

Instead of being enclosed in a maze of paths, with the perfumed scent from so many wet bushes, a widening village street pointed to clear land rising all around. I didn't understand why we weren't together. The stars had seemed fixed for us. I certainly didn't moan about having gone to Stafford for nothing, because who knew that anything was for nothing when you'd had no option but to do it? I had transposed myself from Nottingham so as to see her, and even if every reason had been against it I would have done the same traipse ten times over. That was the way I moved. I couldn't act in any other way. I knew it more than ever the longer I lived, and I also realized that I would never be able to do anything about it.

When I offered my crumpled fags Sheffield took one, but the others didn't smoke. Noah drank lemonade: ' "Don't smoke, don't drink – Norfolk." Get it? When somebody called Alf Norfolk got invited to a party he wrote a letter back and that's what he said in it.'

We laughed so loud – to mock his humour – that a couple of girls looked out of the pub door as if wanting to be let in on the joke. The others wouldn't have minded, and neither would I, but they already had a party of youths with them.

Noah glanced at the girls inside the pub but they showed no more curiosity. 'I bought the tandem so's my sweetheart could come with us, but her mother put her foot down and stopped her.'

'I expect Jack Randall's had a bit of you-know-what at every place he stopped at, though,' Sheffield said. 'He got taken to court last year because he put a tart up the spout, and now he pays eight-and-sixpence a week out of his wages.'

Pete licked the rim of his empty glass. 'He's a toolsetter, so it wain't put him back much.'

'Last year he met a lass at Banbury,' Noah told me, 'so this year he set off three days before us, and headed straight there.'

'I expect he found her,' Pete said. 'Some people have all the luck, though I suppose he works for it.'

Sheffield flipped his fag end onto the road. 'We can't go chasing Jack Randall all over the shop.'

'It's only fifteen miles,' Noah said, 'so let's look him up. We can book our beds in the morning and stay here tomorrow night as well.'

'You'll only find him if you search every hedge bottom with a sharp stick and a flashlight.' Sheffield turned to me. 'Old Jack can hide like a lizard in the bracken. As long as you help us, though.'

'There's a lot of hedges around here.' But I promised to do what I could. We bought our last drinks before getting back for lights out at half past ten, being sure the warden wouldn't let anyone stay a minute beyond time. 'The bogger would lock Gabriel himself out,' Noah grumbled. 'I've seen his sort before.'

Fourth Day

I

After bread and margarine, an apple and some tea, we put on our clips and set off, saying little for the first five miles. Rolls of cloud looked like curlers in the hair of a woman who'd had nothing but worry all her life. Grunts and the shouts of waking-up peppered the raw road. It was as if summer had vanished. Sheffield called out that the beer we'd drunk the night before must have been the lowest grade of sock juice.

I hadn't pedalled down through Derbyshire like they had, so found our route the hilliest yet. I wouldn't come back that way. It was barmy to think I couldn't take another hill, but that's how it seemed. On the map I noted a return route through Adstone and Weedon Beck. Pete argued that it looked just as hilly, as well as a bit longer, but I said at least it was different. 'The same bloody fields, though,' he shot back. 'Nothing but fields. Green misery.'

Sheffield and Noah came onto my side by saying it was best not to cover the same ground twice, a discussion that set us off on a cavalry charge, the tandem up front like a tank.

Locked into myself, I couldn't help wondering about this daft search towards Banbury for a know-all bloke called Jack Randall, when I could have been going through flatter country in the Ely or Bedford direction. Maybe I would have teamed up with someone like Oswestry and talked about politics or geography, whereas a loudmouth who not only smoked, drank, and fucked, but rode five hundred miles and more in the summer holiday, and made every girl pregnant he came across, meant nothing to me. I supposed he even helped blind and crippled people to cross the road, and that when a farmer was late with the harvest Jack Randall turned up and got it in single-handed before the first weighty hailstones came thumping down.

Tracking such a type didn't seem the right object for a push up steep gradients so soon after breakfast. The others thought that by rubbing close against Jack Randall all his prowess would flow into them. They might be right, but who was I to share it? Anything shared wouldn't be worth much, and if it was better than nothing, how much was that worth?

They laid bets on what time the sun would come out, and none of them thought it wouldn't show up at all. Such speculation was a waste of time but I didn't mind being drawn in. Noah decided that half past ten would be about right for a little ray of sunshine.

'That's when it's come out on the last three days, so there's a chance it'll do the same again. Not that I mind whether it does or not. Sunshine means nothing to me. As long as it don't rain, I'm happy. If there's one thing I can't stand, it's rain. I don't mind getting wet, if I have to have a bath, but if the top of my head gets pissed on I get dizzy. Even if I see rain in the distance it upsets me. My eyes start to close, and I want to go to sleep. I don't know why.'

He stopped cycling, eyes bulging like big marbles. I thought he was ready for the asylum, but we gathered round to have a good laugh, and tried to cure him of his barmy notions.

Pete turned to me. 'He always gets over it. Jack Randall used to be a bit like that. But it went, from one day to the next. It'll be the same with Noah.'

We hoped so, and gave him a drink of water because it was time to push on. A horizontal fountain poured from his mouth. He felt better after that.

Sheffield didn't bother to look up before making his bid for the sun. Five minutes to eleven should see the heating on. That's when everything important happened, or was about to, and if nothing did it wouldn't be his fault. Only when no further decision was expected of him did he look guiltily at the dull sky.

Such opinions were no more than guesses, and weren't worth the air they were breathed onto. They couldn't take the place of evidence from scientific apparatus which was capable of producing near certainties. In Nottingham, by 'The Trip to Jerusalem', was a fairground on some bomb-damaged space. Among the stalls and roundabouts was a gaudy machine with a bar in front that you were asked to grip while the lights flashed and told your future – after you had put the required penny in. My mates varied their hold on this hollow bar, as if the difference in pressure would register some alteration to their fortune from the person who had gone before, or get closer to the truth for them alone. Nevertheless, the little printed cards delivered into the slot at knee level were often the same. 'You are firm in purpose and will go a long way. Look after your health' had come up more than once.

They looked at the sky and didn't like what they saw. But clouds were either there, or they weren't. It rained or it didn't, which was all that mattered. Clouds made the sky like a landscape that changed all the time. In meteorology I had learned to recognize every type of cloud from cirrus to cumulonimbus.

Pete Clipstone said the sun would show its face by twelve, if only to make us sweat blood. I threw in my bid for half past four, I didn't know why. If it hadn't come out by then it would be too late, and if it shone afterwards we would have a bonus. Sun in the evening made the day good to look back on no matter what had happened. I didn't really care when the sun came out, or even if it would or would not. I agreed with Noah that what we didn't want was rain. The sun would come out in its own good time, and nothing you could say would alter that fact or make up the sun's mind. 'But rain makes the lorries skid, and if a lorry's got your number on it, there's nothing you can do.'

'It's nowt to do with your number,' said Noah. 'I suppose it's according to whether God wants you or not. If He does, He'll get you – and no mistake.'

'He must be busy up there,' Pete said, 'scribbling all them numbers. It's a wonder He don't run out of chalk!'

'He'd use a pencil,' Noah said, 'not chalk.'

We had a good laugh, biking together, taking up most of the road till the honk of a motor horn sent the tandem wobbling towards the hedge. We were saved from capsizing by a last-minute bit of coordination between the riders. Sheffield shook his fist as the car rounded a bend.

'Jack Randall carries a nice big stone for a thing like that.' Pete pulled strands of grass from between the mudguard and tyre. 'He wouldn't mess about. He'd hurl it through the back window. Not that I wouldn't rather be in a car, though.' He looked wistful. 'One day I'll have a motor, the biggest I can lay my hands on.'

Nobody denied it, which encouraged Sheffield, who giggled as if it was something only a sexual pervert would want. 'I might even have one myself.'

'Jack Randall's satisfied with a bike though,' Noah said, when we stopped at the top of a hill. He bit into a cheese sandwich, but put half of it back into the paper. 'I wouldn't mind a mutton chop for dinner.'

We all laughed.

'You eat meat every day with Jack Randall,' Noah informed us. 'He's that sort. Got to have it. When he took me to Lincolnshire a couple of years ago he caught birds and rabbits. He stood at the edge of a field till they came up to him. He said he'd cut my throat if I didn't be quiet. I just sat and looked. He walked across that field so's even a moth wouldn't hear him.'

'A moth ain't got tabs,' said Sheffield.

'Your mother had, I'll bet,' said Pete.

'Don't say owt about my mother.' Sheffield's face went purple. 'Or I'll kill you. She's dead.'

'I know she is,' Noah said, 'so shurrup. Anyway, a rabbit's got sense. It stopped near Jack, and he went towards it, allus stopping when the rabbit wanted to run away. The rabbit felt safe with Jack. It was a treat to watch.'

'Sounds a good idea,' said Pete, 'but it'd tek ages.'

'Not as long as you'd think. When the bunny felt safe, Jack went a bit closer.'

'He hypnotized it,' Pete said, 'like Bela Lugosi.'

'As soon as he got close he threw a stone and stunned it. Then he jumped on it, and hit it at the back of the neck.'

'A rabbit chop!' Sheffield tried harder than the others to believe in Jack Randall. 'I even saw him do it to a bird.'

'He stuffed it into his saddlebag,' Noah went on. 'He made a fire on the beach. He skinned it and cut it up. We roasted the bits, and boiled some spuds from a field. It was fit for King George to eat.'

'He don't tek anybody with him anymore.' For Sheffield the fact marked the end of a perfect time. 'He wants every floxy he can get, so he goes on his own.'

'That's the only way to do it,' said Pete. 'It's Jack's way.'

'Let's get going, then, or we'll never find him.' I was already on my bike. They would be riding on their own next year. It happened to every gang. I supposed they'd lasted longer than most.

'If he was in the army he'd be in the commandos.' We sat in a field to eat our bread and cheese. They wouldn't leave bloody Jack Randall alone. 'Quiet as a mouse,' Sheffield said. 'Deadly as a tiger. That's Jack. He waint have to go in the army, because he's a toolsetter.'

'They might call him up now the war's over,' said Noah. 'He wouldn't be easy to catch, though.'

Pete passed his flask of tea. 'If I have to go, why shouldn't he?'

The hills no longer deadly, they swapped yarns about Jack Randall's powers for another five miles. I supposed that whether the bloke lived or not, the talk was what mattered. You got hungry, thirsty, wet or puffed out, but it didn't mean much if you had a tale to spin till you could buy a new-baked loaf, find a water tap, or flop onto a flock mattress at the end of the day. All of a sort, the four of us couldn't be friendlier, yet they were conniving in a joke against me, based on the fact that Jack Randall didn't exist. They argued as to whether he had blue, grey or brown eyes, though maybe they had never really noticed. Each put on Jack Randall a wish of their own that they would like to come true, and they were good at it.

The same thing used to go on at school, and even in the factory. Ralph Thomas said that when his father in the army was looking after some German prisoners, one threw acid in his face. The others tried to escape as well, but Ralph Thomas's father stopped them, in spite of his burning skin and the fact that he was nearly blinded. He was given a commission, and a medal for such a brave deed.

'That happened two years ago, and now he's a major,' Ralph told me during our dinner hour. Then I saw Mr Thomas one day when he came to the factory to collect Ralph's wages. It turned out that he had never been in the army. In fact he had just been discharged from prison. I told the others about it.

It all depended on how you told the lie, or joke, or even the truth. Maybe Jack Randall did live, and had been everywhere, like Kilroy. On the other hand maybe he didn't, though whether he lived or not, it wouldn't have been very interesting to meet that sort of bloke.

And we never did catch him up, though we searched page 92, and even a corner of page 93. The warden of the hostel near Banbury said he wasn't sure Jack Randall had stayed the night before, and with a wink urged us to keep on going south-east. Somebody close to that description had left the same morning for a hostel in Buckinghamshire. But that direction was beyond our radius of action. In any case, I wasn't going to spend my holiday searching for Jack Randall. I knew quite a few who lived on our street. Jack Randalls weren't all that rare where I came from.

The market place at Banbury was as far as I could get from Nottingham. I had never been so far south, or north, or in any other direction. Skegness was nearly the same distance, but that was on the coast, so you had to stop whether you wanted to or not.

I was so much out of contact that letters wouldn't find me. Was my mother worried? Not on your life. Nor was I worried about anything. Telegrams would boomerang in the senders' faces after going from pin to pin like a penny through the guts of a slot machine. What would a telegram have said? 'Don't come back. You've got TB.' Or: 'Come back soon, you've got your air traffic control job for a near certainty.' If there had been any real news they would have put out an SOS on the wireless: ' . . . where his mother, father, brother and Aunt Lily are dangerously ill in separate wards of the General Hospital.' I would have stopped my ears, and I took care not to get near a wireless and have my freedom ruined.

To be out of earshot was marvellous, especially when I knew that at home there would be a letter waiting for me from Alice Sands with a photograph inside. I would never forget what she looked like again, between one visit and the next. My impulse was to go straight home, reach there in a day, yet something told me that such a course would be cheating, and I would be paid out by there being no letter from her if I did that. I had to do a proper circuit, the more or less prepared tour, to earn the reward of such a love letter.

II

Lights out seemed too early. Twilight put a cloak over the fields. It was barely dark, and wouldn't take long to get light again. You had to rush through and get your rest, but we couldn't sleep, though a score of others tried and did, till our muttering woke some, who told us to put a sock in it or they'd tell the warden. We nattered about films, and I told them what few books I'd read. I also said I would like to go on biking forever.

'I don't want to go home, either.' Sheffield's real name was Barry Coutts, but it was too late for me to use it.

'You've got to,' Noah told him. 'We've all got to go home sometime or other.'

'And soon,' Pete said.

'I don't care if I never go home.' Sheffield spoke so forlornly that I wondered what was up with him. 'My old lady died last year. She had consumption. I live with an uncle because the old man didn't want me with him. But this bloody uncle's allus getting on at me, and I think I'll do him in one of these days. I will if he don't sto .'

'You'll have to leave home then,' said Noah. 'Live in digs. I would.'

'That's what I'll do,' Sheffield said, as if he would never be able to do anything at all. 'I'll bloody kill him, though, if he don't stop needling me.'

I drifted in and out of their talk, too tired to put my ha'porth in, though I did from time to time. 'What does he needle you about?'

There was a long silence, and I thought everybody had gone to sleep. I was just about to let go of the edge of the cliff when I heard: 'He says I killed my mother, but he's a liar.'

'You don't have to kill *him* though, do you?' Pete said.

'I know, but he says it every time he sees me. So I stay out of the house all I can. But he waits up for me, and shouts at me for being late. Then he says I killed my mother. But my mother allus had consumption. As long as I can remember she had it.'

After another silence he went on: 'My dad was out at work one day, and she was in bed downstairs. She asked me to go to the shop and buy half a pound of filleted cod. She fancied it for her tea. I thought I'd never remember such a thing. "Half a pound of filleted cod!" What the hell was that? I was thirteen, and didn't want to go on the errand. It was a lovely summer day and I wanted to get back in the street. I'd only gone for a drink of water, but she nabbed me. "Half a pound of filleted cod," she said. "That's all I want. Be a good lad, and go and get it from the shop for me." I suppose I was ashamed that she was allus in bed. She hardly ever got out. I said no, and swore at her, and ran into the street. I'd never remember half a pound of filleted cod, I thought. It seems too daft to ask for. By the time I got to the fish shop I'd buy summat else, and that would be worse than forgetting it altogether. Anyway, I didn't know she would die in there in three years time, did I? If I'd known that I would have gone. Anybody can die, can't they?'

'They can,' we mumbled, hoping by now that he would calm down and let us get to sleep. We couldn't nod off while he was like that. 'So I went out, to run around with my mates,' he said, 'and didn't get her that half a pound of filleted cod. I wish I had done, though.'

'It worn't your fault,' Pete said.

'When my uncle called a few days later she must have told him about it. She never told my father. But I was good to her after that, because I knew I'd done wrong. But this bloody uncle never lets me forget it. I'll never forget, anyway, but he lets me have it whenever we're together in the house: "Who didn't go and get his mother half a pound of filleted cod then when she was dying eh? Eh? Eh? Eh?" He'll say it once too often, though, one of these days.'

Pete yawned. 'Why don't you tell him to get stuffed?'

'I'd do it,' Sheffield said, 'but I can't get a word in edgeways when he gets on at me. I just can't bloody speak. He's only a rotten little titch, but if I hit him . . . Well, I don't know. I think I'll kill him.'

I thought he was going to cry, but he belched and

went to sleep, for which I wasn't sorry. I hoped he'd
have good dreams, then he might feel better in the
morning. I wanted to know what time it was, but didn't
have a watch. When a clock struck the time I couldn't
tell whether it was two or three. Alice wouldn't leave
me alone, or I wouldn't leave her alone. We haunted
each other, or at least I hoped she thought so. I slept
like a stone split in two by a sledgehammer. The
patterns were clear and marbled, and red and grey and
purple. My fever tried to stage a come-back, but
towards morning I stopped caring, and opened my grip
on the ropes I had been clinging to, not worried at all
how long the falling would go on.

Fifth Day

I

'I don't care where I go to, as long as I go somewhere,' Noah said while they were cleaning the hostel kitchen.

'We'll get lost after Nottingham peels off,' Pete said as he packed his bags outside. He put a hand on my shoulder. 'The first town we come to I'm going to buy a proper map.'

'I always get lost when I look at a map,' said Noah.

'We'll buy one in Rugby,' said Sheffield. 'We'll club together. It might cost a shilling. How much did you fork out for that atlas?'

'Five bob, I think.'

A lot of fuss was made about giving each other our addresses. Paper was arranged, and a pencil found. They wanted to stay in touch. We were friends forever. Noah buttoned his jacket against the wind. Pete told me how to get to their street, but without a town plan his directions were too confusing. We'll meet in Mansfield for a drink at weekends, Sheffield said, or go rowing on the Derwent at Matlock Bath. Next year in summer we can go to the Lake District. The paper blew away, and he put the pencil back in his pocket. They forgot that me and Pete would be with the colours.

I pushed my bike to a good speed, and then mounted it like a cowboy, setting off by the back road to Weedon Beck so as to side-step the zone of aerials and avoid their influence. I was sorry at not getting their proper names or giving mine. Maybe they were sorry as well, but I was on page 113 and going through Northampton before it occurred to me.

I had also forgotten about going back to Stafford on the off-chance of seeing Alice. By now I was ten miles further along the road. The hour before departure was always blank. I looked forward to the middle of the day, and imagined where I would be at the close. There was nothing to do but keep on. With mud in front and mud behind, you never turned back – or so I once heard a man say at work – though there wasn't any mud at the moment.

I felt an ache as I worked east and an ache as I steered north, head bent to the road whichever direction I headed in, but no ache or pain was serious anymore. Time would make it fade or send it away. I had often had toothache but even that hadn't lasted forever. Something I'd eaten had turned my guts, maybe sour apples overhanging a garden wall on the way into Banbury.

I hardly cared how far on I was to closing the circle that would take me home. Beyond Kettering and Weldon I knew that what I needed most was sleep, feeling as if I hadn't put my head on the pillow for days. I biked like a zombie, knackered without knowing why.

The overcast sky held me to the tarmac ribbon of road unrolling under my wheels like black bandage coming off a mummy fresh out of a coffin, leaving me as if naked in a sharp crosscutting wind. The way was up and down, fields and woods dragging on either side. Isolated houses, or dwellings packed into towns and villages, weren't for me. I had craved one for a refuge, but now I wanted more space than could be found in England. Nor was Rockingham Forest real, because patches of wood on both horizons rarely came down to the road.

At the village of Blatherdene, on page 132, a sign on the gate of a cottage garden said that tea was served there. A couple of chairs and tables were set by an arbour of roses more colourful though less perfumed than those of Wishdale Abbey. The woman, wearing a sackcloth apron, brought out a tray of scones, bread and butter, honey and a pot of tea. I thought it might be expensive, but when she said it would cost a shilling I was pleased it was so cheap.

She had a large bosom and a narrow waist, and was almost as tall as me when I looked at her before sitting down. Her lips were thin and horizontal, but what I noticed were the upper and lower lids of her eyes coming close together, with a slight but obvious slant in both. The colour between was such an icy blue it was almost white. My barefaced gaze was struck by embarrassment, and I told myself not to stare.

Her fair hair swayed behind as she walked away, leaving me to get on with my tea. I had wanted to kiss her, and more, and my hands shook, lifting the willow pattern cup the right way up to pour in some tea. The crockery reminded me of that behind a glass case at home which my mother had brought from my grandmother's house when she died. I had never known her. She had died before I was born, 'of a broken heart', my father said, sounding as if about to cry over it again, 'because of your Uncle Fred. He cut gangways of grief through his family with a knife, that bugger did, and hadn't cared who suffered.'

But my mother had kept all such marvellous cups and saucers, and Uncle Fred had made no trouble about her having them. 'I'll break every bone in his body if he does,' my father said he had said, though I was sure he wouldn't have done anything at all. He never did. He just liked to hear himself talk, making me think that the sooner I got away from home the better.

I was pleased with the abundance of bread and butter, the amount of honey, the ocean of tea. Cycling reduced me to the lowest common denominator. I enjoyed hunger because I had earned it, but also because at that moment it was more a part of me than anything else. I ate and drank as if I had never had enough to eat, which was not true. I just had an appetite for coming back to life.

Beyond the roses was an orchard, myriads of apples on the trees, and beyond were beehives from which came an ominous noise of insects making what I enjoyed eating. The lawn near the windows was covered with yellow flowers, like dandelions though not so big, about six inches tall, and every now and again a bee would hang on the top, its weight almost bending the flowerhead as far as the ground. Then the bee would take off, leaving the flower to spring upright. The whole lawn had these intermittent wobbling flowers where bees were at work. I looked through the book bought in Stafford (at least I had something to remember the place by) and found that they were called Goat's Beard.

A sudden wind made me wonder if a storm wasn't coming. The birds were in turmoil, except for a small thrush hopping across the lawn which, on coming to a dandelion, jumped over because no one had shown it how to go round, and pecked at a crumb I had thrown from the table.

Trees rattled and swayed. Some bees abandoned the Goat's Beard. A wall of greenery hemmed the garden in but on looking up I thought the weather wouldn't change. It wasn't that kind of day. When every slice of bread was finished the woman asked if I wanted more. She had taken her apron off, and looked fine in her

133

white blouse and purple skirt. She wanted to be another person from the one of half an hour ago. Or maybe she was dressed up to catch a bus for Stamford, and I had to make haste and get out.

I thought she had taken pity on me, supplying so much food for a shilling. I couldn't have eaten more, in any case. It would seem too greedy after such a feed. She looked puzzled when I refused, and then asked where I was going. Perhaps she thought I was searching for my long lost relations, or that I was biking to Nottingham to get a job, because I couldn't afford the train. I said I was on holiday, and that I liked going everywhere on a pushbike.

'That's different,' she smiled. 'Do it while you can.'

'It's a nice garden,' I said, when she kept looking at me.

'Ay, and it takes some caring for. But we do our best. My husband helps, except that he works at the farm. He's the manager, and never gets back till late, especially in summer.' She managed the pots onto the tin tray. 'The farm owner would like me to go into the fields and help with the harvest as well. But I told him it isn't wartime anymore. I wasn't cut out for that sort of thing. Before I got married I worked in an office.'

It was impossible not to glance at her unusual eyes, and her large hands as they worked. She smiled at me, and then I saw that her lips had life after all, and that her eyes had more light in them than in those of ordinary shape.

'The whole place takes a lot of work.' She stood with the tray. 'But things'll improve as soon as my son comes back from the navy. I had two, both of them before I was twenty, but one went down somewhere or other.' She named a ship I'd never heard of. 'I don't suppose I shall know where it was. That's the worst of the navy.'

I felt she was going to cry. I hoped not. Her eyes were too good for that. But maybe the best eyes cry easiest. 'The damned war,' she said, 'never did the likes of us any good. Or anybody, for that matter.'

My father had said the same when I went down to the recruiting office. He nearly had a fit, but he couldn't stop me. My mother had cried. I wanted to laugh. Since they couldn't stop me, I was free. I didn't know why, but there was nothing else for me to do except enlist. I was only sorry they wouldn't call me up straightaway. Even to go off and be killed was better than not getting out of the house. All the same, in the last few months, if I cheeked the old man about something he said that I would do as I was bloody well told when I went in the navy. They'd settle me, right enough. Any bloody lip to them, and I would be for it.

'I bore him and brought him up,' she said. 'He was a wonderful boy.'

Hundreds of thousands had been killed, millions all over the world. What could you expect? I thought she wanted to be alone, but I just stood there. I saw myself getting on my bike and setting off, but I didn't move, because I couldn't. The smell of cut grass and mown wheat, roses and fallen apples rooted me to the middle of the earth. Her smile, which I couldn't puzzle out, was a mixture of pain and happiness as she set the tray on the grass between us. A pair of wasps were immediately at the remnants of honey, and my last inclination before she put her arms around me was to wave them away.

'The little devils will sting if you touch them,' she said, her lips smiling and trembling at the same time. 'They're all over the place this year.'

I can't think why, but I tried to avoid the smell of sweat and pepper. If she had been a young girl I'd have

135

loved it. Her breasts were soft and her arms strong, and I couldn't leave her because my cock got as hard as a stick of seaside rock. She kissed me on the ear and on the cheek, and instead of going quietly out of the cottage gate as had been my intention I kissed her right on the mouth because there didn't seem to be any other place close enough. All I thought of was to wonder if she had got false teeth, though I don't think she had. I couldn't think of anything else. No ideas were in my head. They never were at such a time, only the urge to do one thing, make one connection, but she stood holding me and I didn't want to move.

Neither did she, and I thought if I don't go soon I won't find a vacant bed at the youth hostel, but I was balanced by holding and being gripped, and could no more have gone than have died of a heartburst, though my blood was thumping, mostly because the pounding of her chest was setting mine even more on the go.

'The neighbours might see us if we stay here,' she said. It was hard to see how they could, but we held hands in the same way as Alice and I might have done, and walked into the house, me saying to myself that I would get on my trusty old bike otherwise I'd be late. And in any case what's happening? She's too old, I thought. She wasn't, because it didn't matter, and I knew she was lovely and that I couldn't believe what was happening because it all seemed so dreamlike and good, and I thought that if I cared, and I didn't know whether I did or not, there's nothing I could do about it.

I put my other hand down to cover myself, thinking that not only the neighbours but all the world could see it, until a homely smell told me I was inside the kitchen. Over her shoulder on a table by the stove I saw a bread board and tea caddy, and four eggs on a plate, but didn't notice much else because I wondered if her husband was there, though knew he couldn't have been otherwise she wouldn't have brought me in.

'You're a good lad,' she said, and I wanted to laugh at the idea that she thought I might not have done it before, and to stop myself doing so I kissed her again on the lips as we edged through the kitchen to the hearthrug comfort of the front room. I wondered where I was, because I wasn't in my own mind. The world was cut in two from when I biked on and on through the countryside, and when I closed my eyes while kissing her, or when she then kissed me, I saw only the dark road rising and falling in front. I undid my trouser buttons as I got down over her on the floor, she pulling a velvet cushion from the sofa, and putting it under her, and me with the automatic pulling of the single packet from my back pocket and trying to take it out, which she nudged away and shook her head at.

If only she was Alice Sands my life would be finished, I thought. I would pump all my spunk into her and she would have a baby and we would have to get married and that would be the end of that. So I forgot Alice and the world and myself and the road, and she pulled up her skirts and I saw her salmon pink knickers and knew enough to undo the buttons between her legs. But she pushed my hand away and did it herself and there was the smell of furniture polish in the room, and sweat from me after such heavy biking, and she wore some scent and powder which mixed with everything else but after seeing the patch of pale hair at her cunt I looked into her eyes and noticed her upper and lower lids close together with some white in between because she never completely closed them, wanting I supposed to look at me all the time.

The sun came through low windows onto the carpets

137

as she undid her blouse and opened her eyes fully to see that I was missing nothing, me going right in as far as I could get, but when I saw the white of her tits I blocked off the sight by kissing her, and putting my face between, for her long warm cunt was sucking me hard. I looked up to take my mind off too quick an end, and saw nothing but the sunny window with flowers and geraniums rambling and spilling about outside.

I even stopped a while so as not to explode, noticing a small round table with a lace cloth on top and a plant pot in the middle, and two pot dogs with orange noses on the shelf behind.

She pulled me on, and I set in with all my love and strength. She opened her eyes wide to look at me, then reared herself up as if she wanted to get into my belly as well, and shouted: 'Sam! Sam!' – whoever he was, but he wasn't her husband, because if he was he would hear her no matter how far away he happened to be. But at her crying out I thought I needed to hold back no longer. Not knowing my name, she could never call it, anyway. So when I knew I was coming, and that nothing in me or the world would stop it, I put myself to her breasts and let go while pressing and sucking them, saying Alice Sands's name to myself for as long as it lasted, until all of my backbone had gone into her fields and meadows.

I'm sending you into the world, she said, though I don't remember her exact words. They must have been something like that. 'You'd better go now. My husband will be home soon.' She seemed upset at what had happened, but I had done just as much as her. I walked quietly out of the gate. I wasn't going to run. If the husband did come back I felt able to kill him. She came after me, not caring about the neighbours anymore, and put a bag of scones into my pocket. 'Are you all right?'

I laughed 'Yes.'

'Come back, when you're this way.'

'I don't want to go.'

'You've got to.'

I'd only said it to make her feel better. 'All right.'

I wobbled a bit at first as I pedalled away, or so I'd tell Albert. I fucked her blind. She sucked me dry. No you don't, I thought. She was lovely, and you keep your trap shut for ever and ever, Amen. And I knew that I would, or at least for so long that it wouldn't matter.

In the open I slowed down. None of the sleep I'd had since leaving home had been deep enough for rest. The only way to get it was to wake up, an idea which did not make sense. I realized now that I hadn't slept properly since before being born. Sleep I had to have, yet I wasn't sure that it was sleep I wanted. Needing had nothing to do with wishing, but because I couldn't get what I wanted I craved sleep.

Aeroplanes cut through silence, engines revving as if insane. Earthworms could do no such thing. Fish in a river wouldn't be so evident. Birds were too small and quick. But I knew all the aeroplanes, and wanted to follow the track made good of every one. Motor cars were ordinary, and dangerous when they passed me by. I couldn't compete with their advantages, so wanted to be in the sky.

An unpaved lane led off the highway, and I decided to fall. A little way along was a gap in a broad hedge of hawthorn and nettles and Queen Anne's lace, wild roses, elderberry, dock leaves and tall buttercups. They formed a buffer zone between me and the field, cordoning me off from the Ministry of Transport 'A' road.

The corn was high, and I pulled the bike after me as if it was an animal that didn't want to follow. Cows

139

were crying, crows and sparrows producing mayhem near a wood. Shotgun cracks came from the west, and a crowd of rooks swept up like the bristles of a great brush from a clump of trees. After a long piss, eyes half closed, I put my bike flat and lay down, all but invisible. Profound rest came pouring into my veins like blood.

II

A lesser road forked off for Kings Cliffe, and I wended along with the sound of birds never out of my ears. Wheat grew high in a field, a faint rattle of wind catching it into a dance. I sifted an ear between my palms, eating the grains one by one. I don't know why, and I never shall, but as I ambled the almost empty road I recalled opening the newspaper some time in May (a month when even in the factory I think of all the good things of the year) and seeing a double-page picture of the concentration camp at Belsen. I'd got home from work, and my mother set a plate of bacon and beans before me. 'Look in the paper,' she said, 'and see what *they've* done to people.' I couldn't take in what I saw, until I'd pored over it again and again.

Why it flashed so real before my eyes on the road to Kings Cliffe I didn't know, but I supposed that such a picture would be there forever, and could come up at any time. I spat out the grains of wheat, and hardly noticed the next few miles because of naked corpses and skeleton-like people wearing a pyjama-sort of uniform. I felt blighted, as if I was one of them. A cold wind went through my stomach, and for a while I would not have bothered if I had been struck dead.

III

When I booked in at the hostel there was one bed left. The warden said I was lucky. Coming back to life I leaned my bike against the wall and then went out for a stroll. I walked along the streets of the large village, passing the Red Lion. It was almost a small town, houses built with the same sandy-looking stone, each garden cared for as in a picture-book. I thought how I would like to live in such a place for the rest of my life, and found it funny that any pleasant village gave me that wish. I wanted to live in every place, claim every wood or field as my own. But I also wanted to run as far from everything as I could, as if the patch of earth I eventually laid claim to would be where I would die. Luckily I had no option but to go on travelling, feeling regret that I couldn't stay, while the idea of adventure took me over completely.

As I walked I saw nothing, but daydreamed the dream to come true of getting to some far-off part of the British Empire and living a fine life forever. If I had my 'wings' I would buy a seaplane and fly people and baggage from one jungle island to another. I almost bumped into the door on getting back to the hostel. Vegetables and bacon cooking at ranges in the kitchen didn't make me hungry enough to want supper. Each of the woman's scones reminded me so much of her body that I wanted to race back there. The husband was at home, or I would have done so. I thought that if she hadn't had a husband I would have stayed for a while and looked after her garden. I also knew I was on the move and couldn't stop anywhere.

There was nothing to be done. The world was an

iron bar you couldn't bend. Nobody could. So I sat in a common-room armchair browsing through the book on wild flowers, savouring names such as mallow and stitchwort, chickweed and campion, sorrel and crowfoot, dropwort and saxifrage, trefoil and yarrow, hemlock and clover, fleabane and furze, groundsel and celandine, agrimony and vetch, chicory and flax, pansy and loosestrife, bindweed and pimpernel, bugloss and lavender, burdock and bryony, scurvy grass and creeping lady's-tresses, goutweed and mousetail, misletoe and marigold – thinking how I might one day tell a story and use them for people's names.

Having finished the flowers I got down to reckoning how many miles I had ridden since leaving home. So much thumbing through the pages of the atlas had weakened the spine, but I totted up two hundred miles, and would add another fifty by the time I got back. To go that far in a straight line would have put me into France, or near Edinburgh in Scotland. No distance seemed beyond me, even under my own power. It was twenty-five thousand miles round the world, and at that rate I could do it in two years, getting a boat across the Pacific Ocean from China to America, and over the Atlantic from America to England.

After two pints of beer and a bag of crisps in the Red Lion I walked back to the hostel. As soon as I closed my eyes at lights out it seemed as if there were gun flashes all over the sky, though without the noise. I went to sleep thinking of the woman who had given me such a big tea for a shilling which she hadn't even collected, and wondering if she was thinking of me. I wanted to send her a telegram to say Thank you, but her husband might be in when it came and he would black her eye in the ructions that followed. Perhaps I would write a letter, though the same things could happen after he picked it up from the mat. It would be best to do neither. I didn't have her address, or even a name. In any case I felt sure she was thinking of me, confusing me with Sam while I was mixing her in my dreams with Alice Sands.

Sixth Day

I

The day lit its way in and prodded me to get up. After a long night's sleep my bed still felt fresh. I could have gone on forever, but people stamped by, to whiffs of carbolic and the swish of towels. Someone dropped from the top bunk like a big white whale.

I felt under my palliasse to make sure the atlas was in its place, then reached my trousers from the hook. The third button up from the bottom had come loose, so I pulled it off. A piece of rag in my bag held needle and cotton, part of the kit list for going to annual camp. The light was dim but the cotton threaded at my second try, and I bodged up as good a job as I could, using such a lot of cotton that the button would stay on even when the trousers around had fallen to bits. Then I yanked myself out of bed and got them on. There was a hole in one of my socks but, as it didn't show, I would darn it when I got home.

In the ablutions I waited for a place so as to have a shave. It wouldn't be good to get home looking like a tramp. The water was cold but my brush and soapstick worked up a good lather. A bit of care, and my skin was smooth except for a nick under the chin. A scrap of newspaper held on for a couple of minutes congealed the blood, so that it didn't look as if I had tried to cut my throat and missed.

Half an hour later I was ready for the road. My intention was to dawdle, so as not to reach home too early in the day. Yet I had to get back soon to read the three letters that would be waiting for me. A middle-aged man, cocking his leg onto a tall bike by the gate, asked where I was going. When I told him, he said: 'I'm off to Nottingham as well. Would you like me to accompany you?'

He had probably spent the night at the hostel. Not that he was much of a youth, being about fifty. He wore a cap, and had glasses, and didn't fasten his trouser bottoms with a pair of clips but with black ribbons, as if somebody in the family had died.

People couldn't bear to see you on your own, and in any case he put his proposal in a very funny way. I wanted to be by myself, ride at my own pace. From Workers' Playtime and Music While You Work I wanted to sneak off into the woods. I was nobody's shadow, never noticing my own. By myself I could see more, stop when I liked, eat when I felt the urge. The old bloke was probably a teetotaller, anyway, and might not even come into a pub for some lemonade. At the bottom of a hill I wouldn't have to beat my guts out to catch him up, or hang back so that he could come level. I had ridden with Oswestry, but that was different.

Nevertheless, the old man stayed with me for a mile or two. I didn't own the road. He was the sort of person with glasses who seemed to see even less when they had them on. His big heavy bike had a case around the chain, and looked more like a tank. A mackintosh was tied neatly on top of his bulging saddlebags, and when he sat upright he towered above the hedges. If I made a run for it he would see me for miles. He rode like a human conning tower.

I had nothing to say, which was my normal state, but if the man wanted to talk he was welcome to while the road was level. I had worked out a way on the map to get to Nottingham without going through Stamford, and the man thought I had taken the wrong turning. I would go via Colly Weston and Ketton, and then Hambleton. Maybe he wanted to visit Stamford, which had a long history. He seemed to be taken with such things, and perhaps thought he would show me an ancient building or two. But I wasn't interested, because I knew my way and that was all I cared about. He stayed close, and said when we got to the top of a rise: 'Did you hear the results of the General Election, lad?'

I didn't like being called 'lad', but told him that I had. There was a smile on his thin, wide lips. 'Don't you think it was good news?'

I supposed it was. Most of the blokes in the factory would think so, not to mention a lot of people in the street.

He took out a white handkerchief and blew his nose. 'That's jolly good, kid! I wish I could say the same about the types who work in our office, or some of the toffee-noses who live in Wollaton Vale.'

I found it hard to believe he had ever been in an office, unless it was to stand inside the door and ask for his wages. As for Wollaton Vale, I knew what he meant, but they were the kind of new houses I could hardly expect my family ever to live in, though I wouldn't mind if they did.

'We've just been through some historic times,' he said, 'you and me.'

As if I didn't know. I'd heard the guns, and the bombs whistling down. But I'd lived through them alone, and not with him, or anybody. All times were historic. They were bound to be, and people lived through them because they had no choice. The longer they lived, what's more, the more history they lived through.

'And now things are going to *alter*.' He giggled with excitement, as if he might be able to do something about changing them. 'Especially for the working man. I can't tell you how pleased I am.' He didn't look it. He looked as miserable as sin. Perhaps he felt glum at not getting much response. 'I've got to tell somebody, anyway, lad. Half the country's voted Labour, and I can't find anybody who did! I expect they're all overseas with the army and navy.'

I wondered if I would be able to shake him off for the next forty years. What did he know about the working man anyway, if he didn't work in a factory? 'You were too young to vote,' he informed me, 'but you won't be at the next election. The country'll get better and better. We'll make Labour's landslide this time look like a few cobbles falling out of a dustpan!'

He supposed my laugh to be from happiness at the idea of being able to make a cross on a piece of paper. As if there weren't more exciting things to do in the world. Next time seemed centuries away. I was only interested in next week, or next year at the most, and in whatever might happen that I couldn't yet know about.

He cranked himself up a slope. 'We've got the whip hand now. The country's changed gaffers, lad, and it's not before time. What an alteration we've got on our hands!'

'I haven't noticed much.'

'Ah, but it's early days. You'll see. It'll never be like it was before the war again. No more unemployed, lad, believe you me. We've done with all that.'

He said nothing for a while, and neither did I. Clouds were piling up, and the wind was against us. A bit of sun still flickered at our eyes. 'You don't mind me riding with you, do you?' he said. 'Because if you do, just say so. I'll understand.'

I wondered how he imagined an old chokka like him could get my goat. 'I don't mind at all.'

'I'm sure you don't. You're far too intelligent-looking for that. I could tell a mile off what sort you are. My name's Tom Clifford, and I'm on a cycling tour. I've been to Kings Lynn and Cromer.' There was a pause, laid out neatly so that I could tell him where I had been. I did.

'That's a damned good itinerary. I'll do it myself one day. On my own, though. I always do it on my own. My wife can't come on such jaunts because she's been bedridden for the last four years. It's ever since the air raids. Once a year her sister looks after her for a week or two while I get out on my own. Otherwise I'd go crackers. Even if she was fit I suppose I'd have to get out on my own, come to think of it. No man is an island, lad, but he's got to act like he is now and again, and see a bit of nature. Don't you think so? We're all part of nature, after all.'

I said that was true, right enough, but still couldn't make out why he was talking to me like this. Fortunately he got puffed out and wasn't able to say much more, though I felt sorry for him and his bedridden wife. 'What's wrong with her?'

He laughed, but not at anything funny. 'She's incurable.' After a dozen revolutions of the wheels he added: 'Like bloody life itself, if you'll forgive the swearing.'

It may be for you, I thought, but not for me. If it was, I'd do myself in – or go to Australia.

'After the war to end wars,' he said, 'the second one I mean, we won't be able to take another, not like this damned packet.' He got off his bike at the top of a slope and looked at the land. Then, and I'll never know why, he began laughing. He laughed at the sky, showing his teeth like a donkey, though they were false. Then he turned and laughed at a great elm near the corner of a field.

I got off my bike. The noise could be heard for fifty miles, but there was something about the laugh that I liked. It said something, though I didn't know what, except that it helped him to live. Without it he wouldn't be the man he was, and it was obvious that he owned his laugh more than anybody had ever owned anything. It must have had his dotty and particular stamp, and he knew it, judging by the way his eyes sparkled. He was his own wild animal in his own private circus, an animal that could never get out of the ring because he had mastered it completely and learned how to live with it. And while he had, it was safe and so was he, even though he looked a bit to somebody like me as if he was barmy. And if by any chance he did let go of the laugh it would always come back to him, though it would be best if it didn't stay away too long otherwise he might think it had got lost. Then he would really go off his head and murder the first person he saw.

But the laugh went on too long and I got embarrassed. I couldn't help feeling sorry for him, and felt better when he stopped. He was more out of breath than from cycling. I pretended to look at my atlas, and heard his clear tone taking on the accent of Alvar Liddel: 'Do you know the greatest disaster of modern times?'

I felt like telling him to mind his own business, and to stop getting personal. I wanted to laugh as well, but not at anything funny. There was a space in my stomach, and I hoped the laughing man would vanish. In Victor Hugo's novel he walked off the deck of a ship in a storm and drowned. Maybe this bloke laughed while he was at home as well, and his wife and the neighbours were glad to get rid of him. Laughing Tom, they called him. He's gone on holiday. Let's hope he don't come back till next year. Still out of breath, he looked at me, and took off his glasses to clean them, as if to give time for my answer. But I didn't have one, and never would have, even though I knew some history. I said nothing, letting him conclude if he liked that I was no more than an ignorant youth.

'I'll tell you. But you must never forget it. Promise?'

He imagined a nod of my head. Promise and run, I thought.

He took off his cap, showing that he was bald. 'It's this, then: that Napoleon didn't invade England in 1804. See what I mean? If he had done he would have brought freedom, equality and brotherhood to this damned country of ours. That's been our trouble. Everything was lost from that minute on.'

Maybe he wasn't barmy, though my knowledge of history wasn't good enough to argue or contradict. Fascinated, I cocked up my ears for more.

'Remember that, lad.' He smiled, as if by talking to me he had done his good deed for the day. I got on my bike. I'd had enough. A soldier back from Dunkirk had given me a coin; and the words in French had been stamped round its rim: *Liberté*, *Egalité*, *Fraternité*. You had to take notice. Maybe he was right. There were lots of ways to learn foreign words, which were just as interesting as English. From looking at maps of South America and finding in dictionaries the meanings of place names that puzzled me, I also knew about the Rivers of January and Silver, the Beautiful Horizon and the Land of Fire, the White Bay and the Vale of Paradise, Sandy Point, and the City of Peace.

He stood by his bike, waving his cap. 'The English

are a nation of slaves,' he shouted. 'Slaves, I tell you! Bootlickers!' For a while he didn't see me. He was shouting at himself. 'Bloody slaves! They'll never learn, never, never, never!'

The same words clattered out, over and over again, and it was impossible not to listen. He stopped as suddenly as he had begun, then came level and rode by my side as if not only was his raving a thing of the past, but as if he had never given in to it. The raver was someone he also had wanted to escape from, and there was relief on his face at the idea of having done so. He smiled, with hardly a care in the world, and pedalled along singing 'Linden Lea' at the top of his voice.

My life's ambition came back, which was to get away from him. If we went through a village people might think he was some mad uncle whose keeper I was. In any case, I didn't feel like a slave, but if I was I didn't want to be told what I could find out for myself and try to do something about. Neither did I want to be a slave to the man's words, true or not. At Colly Weston crossroads he was undecided which way to go, so I went left and launched myself with the same desperate speed as when I had been threatened by the man on the horse at Loxley. Tom Clifford on his tank-bike could make up his own mind which route he wanted, and catch me up if he could.

A mile later I forked right, along a lane between open fields, then crossed the main road by a pub called The Cavalier. I zoomed through Colly Weston and down two hundred feet of hill towards the River Welland like a bird wanting to alight on the view below. When the lane narrowed, elderberry branches held out clusters of blossoms like ornamental plates. I stood on a low stone rampart, interested in how water flowing under the bridge made the scenery greener in the distance, and hoping the barmy old ranter on the high bike wouldn't charge down and buttonhole me with another history lesson.

After the station, and an inn not yet open to serve even shandies, the lane went between the sandstone walls and houses of Ketton village. I was sorry I hadn't done more navigation off main roads, so as to come across many such beautiful places, though I didn't want to live at this one but pedalled upwards with trees on either side, the lane then going like a tubular track through the middle of the wood itself, clouds of sparrows lifting at my advance.

On the main road at Empingham stood the White Horse. One snug pub came after another, but all doors were closed. My ankles ached where the clips rubbed, so I got off to adjust them. I could stop when I liked, no hurry now I was going home. I didn't want to get there, yet couldn't resist the pull, though knowing that some day it had to be broken.

I opened my atlas even more often than necessary so as to slow down, and noticed a couple of miles south-west a village called Edith Weston, which set me to wondering what kind of a woman or girl she was. It could be – for a start – that 'Colly' Weston was her father, a hedger and ditcher who'd made a small fortune during the war selling poached rabbits. But no, I decided, she would have to have a better old man than that if I was to find her interesting.

The thinning clouds were whiter, sun over most of the land and turning the green pale, but I knew I would never meet Edith Weston, and would have to imagine her if I was to know anything about her at all, though I didn't know why I had to know, just because her name was on the map. Still, it wasn't every girl who had her name on the map.

Her hair would be almost black, and, unlike asphalt on the road, there were natural waves that fell down her shoulders. Her grey eyes, turning green, presented her with more than she looked for, which gave a surprised expression, and put a sly smile on her well-shaped lips. If I knew her all my life I would never properly know her. That was the sort of woman I wanted to know. But I didn't see how I could ever meet her if I didn't know what to expect beforehand, which was why I had to think about her till I saw her as if she had just been one step to the side of me all her life.

Her body I didn't see. I find it hard to think of a woman's cunt if I'm in love. I just want to get into her. Only her face contained her spirit, or whatever it was that made me think about her, the one thing that would help me to remember her. Maybe her name wasn't Edith Weston. What's in a name? She could have any, but such a name called whoever she was to mind, and set me to finding out who she was and what she was like.

She smelled of the perfume of roses, and fields of freshly cut wheat. She smelled of the air, and the reek of petrol as a lorry went by. When she held her cut finger over a brook blood fell into the frog spawn, and the two liquids meeting had a smell like nothing else on earth because the earth itself was made out of it. Everything was something to remember her by. Yet it was possible she didn't live in this area, in spite of a village bearing her name.

I was tempted to take a left-forking lane and see if I could discover her house. The shape and size and situation might tell me more about her. But I didn't turn from the main road because I knew there would be nothing to learn in the locality of the village unless her mother or grandmother stood before me in the queue at

153

the local shop and happened to be talking about her to the woman behind the counter. There wasn't much chance of that. If there was I might hear how she had disappeared one night when nobody was looking. She had gone off to join the Land Army. She lay dead in the bushes, saturated with rain. Or she had become a schoolteacher in Wales. She was a prisoner in Hong Kong. She worked on munitions at a place near London. There was no saying where she would be. Perhaps she didn't even know herself – wherever she was. Maybe she owned a house and sat looking onto a lawn fresh with daisies.

By now she had gone to a part of the world where, if ever I saw her, I'd be so tongue-tied that it would be better we'd never met. But even if we hated each other at first sight my whole belly craved a glimpse, and I hoped to one day bump into her if only because I thought I never would.

I wanted to see into the future by pressing hard on the pedals going uphill before Oakham, as if to mill its moving pictures from the tarmac. Maybe she hid in the woods to one side or the other, but the future was a glass wall, castle-thick, continually in front and shifting away as I moved forward, a mirror in which I could see my own face and the grid-bike I was riding but nothing else.

Turning back to the scenery, I felt myself lapped in all kinds of green and, effortlessly riding onto page 131, tried to wipe the mirror clean in front of my eyes. I'd never been able to see my own face so plainly before. One way to get rid of it was to relive my encounter with the woman in Blatherdene whose son had joined the navy and drowned. Was I going into the navy so that I would drown? You could only think of one thing at a time. Two pictures wouldn't mix. They dazzled around and fought until one won. The drowning sailor felt his eardrums burst, and then his lungs as he went too far down ever to get back up again. I centred my handlebars and pedalled faster. The notion pushed Edith Weston out of my mind.

A large manorial house of grey stone on a hill top looked as if made of the blocks we played with in the infants' class. The school was surrounded by main roads, and grown-ups living nearby called it Crying Island. I whizzed downhill, fish ponds on my right, till the first houses of Oakham came in sight.

Back into myself, speeding by the Crown Hotel, a policeman looked as if thinking I had pinched the bike I rode, but soon I was climbing up and out, and steaming homewards on the A606 with thirty miles to go. High clouds were piled white, and a rumble of thunder came from God's guts. I hoped it would stay no more than a threat in the east, because brakes when wet could make you skid in the rain, and there were steep hills between me and Trent Bridge. It was so warm I took off my coat and tied it across the saddlebag with a piece of string.

II

The Wheatsheaf, set on a bend of the road, was just opening its doors. An old man already sat at a table, and I couldn't see how he had got in before me. Maybe he had been there since last night. Or from tiling the roof he had slithered down the chimney as soon as the first bolt rattled. The large pipe he puffed had a bowl so cracked it looked as if it had been found during an earthquake. He took it out of his mouth, tossed a blob of his spittle into a corner, where it probably crushed a spider to death, and eyed me in the sure knowledge that I still had six months to go before my eighteenth birthday, and that if I didn't get out quick I would spend three of them in prison for illegal drinking. But the man behind the bar, not caring what age I was, filled the pint jar nine-tenths with beer and put in the barest dash of lemonade to make a perfect shandy.

'Come far?' the old man said.

I turned from leaning on the bar. 'Not too far.'

He wore a cap, a suede waistcoat with a gold watchchain between two pockets, and a collarless shirt. His unlaced boots stuck out from under the table, showing white ankles. He had no socks on. 'How far's that, then?'

'I haven't reckoned it up yet. My milometer broke.' I drank half the jar at one go. It tasted of soap, but was delicious. I would have given him the spare socks out of my saddlebag, except that they stank. In any case he looked a different man on Sunday, dressed in his best for church. His married sons and daughters were terrified of him, but his grandchildren thought he was king of the village, if not of the whole world. They loved him because, when he'd had a pint too many – which was almost never – he was free with his pennies. 'I'm heading for Nottingham.'

A sickle gleamed by his pewter tankard. 'Terrible place. Wouldn't go there if you paid me.'

I didn't think anybody was likely to, at his age. He was only an old man, after all, in spite of the jewel-like glint in his eyes.

'Have you got a racing bike, then?' he snapped after a while.

I didn't know whether I annoyed him more by speaking, or by keeping quiet. 'No,' I was glad to admit, 'just an old cronk.'

156

'I was thirty before I had a bike.'

That was because they hadn't been invented then. He was older than Methuselah. 'You don't say?'

'I do. I was married, and couldn't afford one. Before then I walked everywhere. I traipsed to Leicester many a time.'

'Leicester's the worst dump in the country.' I was close enough to home not to give him the pleasure of treating me like an outsider. 'There's nowt to do there.'

'That's as maybe,' he said testily.

'I suppose it is a long way from here, though,' I admitted.

'Damn near eighteen miles. And we'd go there and back in a day. No motors then.' The laugh rattled his false teeth. 'We took a few short cuts along the footpaths, mind you. We had legs like pistons. Iron hard. Mile after mile through the fields. Mud up to our knees, sometimes. They was good days, though, them was.'

If he tried it now his bare white ankles would crack in half a mile. The old chokka read my mind: 'I could still do it, even though I am seventy. I'll bet I could walk any young 'un off his feet.'

Perhaps he could, but he was a boastful old bastard. Maybe he couldn't. A bloke in the factory was always boasting about what he could do, but we found out he'd been telling the truth. So you never knew what to believe. The old man gave two smart knocks on the wood with his empty tankard, and the publican, recognizing the signal that had probably resounded for sixty glorious years, and worn holes in half a dozen tables, came speedily from the back of the pub to prove that he also was still a young 'un. He took it without a word, and refilled it in double-quick time. 'Here you are, Mester Close.'

'Don't think I've ever walked more than ten miles at one go,' I said.

He cackled. 'That's because you never needed to. Have you? Go on, admit it, then.'

'But I've ridden eighty miles on a bike.'

'It ain't the same. But I expect it teks some doing.'

'It was dead easy,' I told him. 'I could do it every day for a month if I had to.'

'Happen life'll be easier now you've got them Labour chaps in gover'ment. Maybe things'll come off the ration, I don't think. We'll still be rationed in ten years with that Attlee bloke. You've only got to look at his face. The sourest phizzog I ever saw. They'll give us a rough ride, let me tell you.'

I'd had enough of the old tike. What did he expect? The moon for breakfast? 'Things'll be different, anyhow,' I couldn't help saying. 'Blokes won't go back to being on the dole like before the war.'

'We shall have to wait and see about that.' There was no stopping him. His face was at least as crabbed at Attlee's. 'I was never on the dole. Too busy working, me. I always worked and always will. Most people don't want to, though, and that's the trouble. Anyway, life won't be much different. We'll still have to work, same as we always did. I'm not that daft. They can't fool me.'

I wanted to be sick, and didn't know whether it was due to his attitude about everything, or because of the shandy. He looked at me, so I stared right back into his white-grey eyes. He was taking the piss out of me, so I didn't care whether his opinions did have any truth in them. I stopped myself telling him that the English were a nation of slaves because I wasn't sure whether I believed it or not. I drained my jar and said I had to be going.

'Good luck to you then,' he chimed. 'I hope you're having a nice holiday. I expect you've earned it. You've got good weather, any road up.'

'Thanks.' I was astonished to see that he had already drained his second pint and was tapping the wood for another. When he pissed, the Ark was launched in the insect world. I couldn't get out fast enough, though part of me felt a definite pull to stay and listen for as long as the old sod could go on talking, though if I matched him jar for jar I would be under the table first.

Shandy plus heavy weather equalled a headache, which was otherwise no bother now that I was in the open air. Thunder stayed at a distance as I pushed up the hill by Holbeck Lodge, freewheeled down into the vale, climbed once more, and again descended. Sheep, sheep, sheep were on either side of the road, nibbling their fields, speckling the up-and-down of the undulations. Leaving Rutland, I clipped a corner of Leicestershire, the smell of fresh-cut grass coming from all directions.

The winding road made me weary, and the weather weighed me down, but being so close to Nottingham it was a case of pressing on regardless, a magic phrase that always helped when energy was low. During my first days in the factory one of the older men, on seeing me flag, had told me to 'press on regardless' and also, in the same breath, to 'make it pay!' His advice helped more than he knew. It stiffened my backbone after the first week, so that nothing seemed difficult anymore – not in the factory, anyway. But that week had been as long as a year.

A carefree ride down into Melton Mowbray took me over the stream and by the railway station. I passed the Boat Inn and the Harborough Hotel, and joined a queue outside a fish and chip shop. The smell tingled my nostrils as if I hadn't eaten for days, and I wanted something to sop up the broiling shandy.

A woman told a soldier who was larking about in front to have more sense and stop pushing. He was short, had fair crinkly hair but was going bald, and had dark shadows under his eyes. He answered that he'd never had much sense, or he wouldn't be dressed in khaki. He wouldn't put up with being ordered about by a bad-tempered spirit like her, either. He was a private in the Royal Engineers, and his tall thin mate was a lance-corporal. Both had the Europe ribbon and the North Africa Star on their tunics. The lance-corporal pushed him, and he pushed the lance-corporal.

They laughed, and I couldn't see what the joke was. If the queue didn't move soon I would ride on and buy a couple of cakes or a loaf at a baker's. 'You was pushing, though, wasn't you?' the woman said.

I'd never seen anyone with such a thin face. She was young, but her skin was lined, and white like lard. She coughed whenever she spoke, either because she was nervous or because she had to, reminding me that I still hadn't heard about my X-ray. I wished she would shut up with her tin-like bark. The shorter soldier couldn't leave her alone. 'Of course I was pushing. I'll push again if I like.'

Maybe he and his mate had been drinking. 'I don't mind you larking about,' the woman said. 'But not pushing.'

I stood without losing my place in the queue, but away from the plate-glass window. The argument seemed six of one and half a dozen of the other, but if the swaddies got funny I suppose I would have to stick up for the woman. 'You shouldn't push,' she said. 'You'll break somebody's basin.'

The two soldiers and other people in the queue

160

laughed, and she turned away, spots of beetroot on her cheeks. 'I didn't know it was funny, did you?'

The other woman, who was wearing a turban, dodged the spray of her coughing. 'You know what sowjers are. Daft as a flight of bees.'

Walking to the marshes beyond Lenton when I was twelve, I saw hills behind the Trent in the distance. By the bridge was a sandbag emplacement with a soldier inside. A Lewis Gun pointed upwards, in case German raiders came over, or paratroops dropped from the sky. One Lewis Gun for the whole of south Nottingham! The soldier was frozen. He wore a balaclava under his tin hat, and battledress and mittens, and told me and Albert to go and get lost when we burst out laughing. What could *he* do about it?

'We don't sting though, missis,' the tall swaddie said in a tone that turned everyone more friendly. 'Not our own sort, anyway.'

'It's more than you dare do,' she said to them.

The hissing of chips in scalding fat came from inside the shop, and when I got my sixpennorth of dinner I straddled the bike and tucked away every last scrap of batter. The soldiers walked across the road and up the street towards the railway station, and the woman coughed her way home with a basin of chips.

I passed the Crown pub, and a row of houses called Belmont Villas, owned by Bertie, I supposed, who lived off what rents he collected. Maybe he'd got lots of such places, and went to Nottingham every night on the razzle. He certainly wouldn't go to Leicester if he wanted a good time. Perhaps the houses weren't owned by him, and they were only called Belmont because, after cycling along the blossom-lined road, I went up a hill that was beautiful enough.

A long flight down took me to a place called Ab

Kettleby, and by a palace of booze and sweet dreams called the Sugarloaf. Nor could I help but wonder who Ab Kettleby was, though I was sure he had never walked in a monastery garden. The road was lined with people when I looked at place names on the map, real faces staring from fields but vanishing as soon as I looked back at the road.

I didn't see why Ab Kettleby should be left out of the game. He was the card of the locality who travelled the world and lived on his wits. He had never done a good day's labour in his life, and though I had worked from fourteen I didn't begrudge anybody their idleness. If Kettleby wasn't able to laze and skive what hope was there of me doing the same if ever I wanted to? Idle people make me laugh, not mad. In any case I supposed that even Kettleby – with his jaunty cap, and thin cigar which was often unlit (too often for him), with his fancy tales and eyes a-twinkle – had done a share of labour in his time, even if only in jug when he had been caught now and again at his tricky antics.

Such goings-on had broken his father's and especially his mother's heart, and many was the time they pleaded with him to reform so that he wouldn't die in a dustbin. When they kicked the bucket who would have the goodness to look after him? I almost cried for the poor bloke while pedalling through the village, though Kettleby would only crow with laughter at such soft feelings. He knew the price of freedom, none better, and expected he would one day have to pay the full amount, but in the meantime he would go his own sweet way, never without half-a-crown in his pocket, though often there was far more jingling coin than that.

A horse whinnied from the hedge and asked for sugar. It's on the ration, mate. Larks flitted everywhere. A cow asked Ab Kettleby to come home. Sheep cawed as if knowing how they were going to die, though not the reason why. Maybe Ab Kettleby married Edith Weston and they lived happily ever after. That would get rid of the pair of them. I almost choked at the thought, and when Kettleby's forlorn face took on the features of Uncle Fred I stopped speculating. Such yarns could only go so far, though it was certain that Ab Kettleby was a more interesting character by far than Jack Randall.

It was no use caring. Wherever you be, let your mind go free. I did, anyway, because if that was the direction I was going I could do little about it except keep on keeping on with all boilers steaming. But I also thought it best to hold myself in check as long as I could, the two most valid mottoes of advice that came from my backbone being to keep reined in, and press on regardless.

I laughed. It was all very well, but from pedalling along, and hardly needing to look at the road, I felt like a biking skeleton, bones between my legs bumping with every inch of the way, an ominous clatter telling me I was riding on the rims of the wheel because I had got a puncture. I swerved into the hedge.

On the last day, it had to happen, though any place was bad enough, and any time galling. I dismounted, and felt that the back tyre was as flat as a pancake, meaning I'd have to get the chain off and the whole wheel out. I stared along the road as if to see what tack or thorn or shard of almost invisible glass I had gone over. If found I would crush it flat. In adversity the world was threatening me – though I knew it wasn't.

I had once cycled fifteen miles on a flat, not having even a pump, and found the inner tube and tyre in ribbons by the time I got home. The present puncture could be mended, however, because I had tools, patches and glue. The easiest way to locate the hole was to pump up the inner tube, put it in water, and watch where the bubbles came from. There was no pond or stream nearby but I saw a farm not too far off, and pushed the bike there.

Chickens clucked from their diamond wire boxes across the yard as I went to the door and knocked. There was the grunt and stink of pigs, the lowing of cows, the cooing of doves. It was a place of rich pickings, where ration books were probably put in a cupboard and forgotten, except for sugar and tea.

There was no answer at the door, but from one of the sheds, above the half gate, was a forlorn face with a black and swollen eye. A piece of dirty plaster hung from a cut on his cheek, and his lips were like two bloated bloodsuckers. The gaze from his steady blue eyes was sad and defiant at the same time, as if he wanted to let me know that he had seen better days, which wouldn't be difficult if you considered how bad this one obviously was.

There must have been some rain, judging by the amount of mud up to the doorstep. 'Is anybody in?'

He put on a smile. Though he had been through a lot of suffering, he was the sort to show it as little as possible. 'Missis gone shop. Back soon.' He opened the half-door and came out, hands holding onto his thick fair hair. 'What you want?'

Anybody would feel sorry, so I took out my cigarettes and offered one. 'I'd like a bowl of water, please.'

The missis hadn't gone shopping. In reality, he had murdered her, and I had caught him at a bad moment, burying her arms and legs in the cowshed. He'd boiled and eaten the head already. But she had given almost as good as she had got in the terrific struggle, though now that the deed was done I looked for the glint of a murder blade half sinking in the mud. I wanted to get on my grid and flee, but before lighting his cigarette he ran into the house and came out with a mug of water, which he held at arm's length. 'Drink!'

I thanked him. Then he took a lighter from his overall pocket and lit our cigarettes. We stood looking at one another. He blew smoke into my face. 'Good!'

'Good fags.' I asked myself who the hell he was. He couldn't be a German prisoner because he would speak better English. 'You work here?'

He growled, took a few quick paces away and shouted:

'No! Yes! No! Work!' His waving arms looked as strong as tree trunks in spring. I was scared and, so as not to show it, lifted my bike, set it down on saddle and handlebars, and began getting the tyre off with my levers.

He calmed down as he watched my activity. 'Me Ukrainian man. Work here.'

'That's good,' I smiled.

'No like work here. Missis no good. Fuck missis.'

I laughed at his vivid telegraphic speech. His laugh was like a coughing fit. He knew I was laughing at him, but didn't mind. He liked it, in fact. I'd never seen anyone with such menacing features and at the same time so good-natured. In some ways his head was noble. Without his injured face he was probably handsome.

'Me fight other Ukrainian men. Much blood.'

He hit me on the shoulder so that I nearly shot over the bike. No one in the factory had ever given such a friendly blow, and I clenched my fists ready to hit back should it be the preliminary to something serious. But another laugh proved that all was well, and in any case

165

I had already got the wheel off and the inner tube out, so thought it best not to show anger. 'You go back to Ukraine, then?'

There seemed more blood pumped into his face than ever. One of the cuts opened. I could tell he didn't intend to go back, ever. 'Stalin kill everybody. Stalin – bad.' He began to cry. 'Me no go. Wife dead. Germans kill. Kiddies dead. Me dead.'

I gave him another cigarette. He was really off his head. Joe for King, blokes in the factory said. One or two of them. Without Stalin we would have lost the war, they told me. I pumped up the inner tube, and heard the hiss of escaping air. I looked up. He had fetched another mug of water. 'Drink!'

I didn't have any fags left, which was a good thing, otherwise I would be pissing all the way home. I drank, and he stopped crying. He smiled. 'You go long way?'

'Nottingham.'

There was a glaze of beatification on his face: 'Nottingham – GOOD!'

I agreed, for form's sake, and asked for a *bowl* of water. He must have thought I had just come out of a desert, for he put a hand above his eyes and looked at the horizon as if to see sand dunes and palm trees. I heard a clatter, and a rusty pump going by the side of the house, and he came out with an enamel bowl slopping over, which he put into my hands instead of on the floor, and looked earnestly as if I might be persuaded to change my mind about becoming known as the greatest water drinker in the world.

I cut my story short, and assumed he knew all along what I wanted the water for. He watched me locate the leak in the inner tube, mend it, and fix everything in place. He drew his fingers along the spokes as if the wheel was a harp. I was attaching the pump back on the frame when I heard a woman's voice shout:

'What's going on here?'

Her hair was curled in front and rolled at the back. She looked about fifty, a broad forehead coming down to a narrow but double chin. She wore brown polished shoes, a long skirt, and white blouse with a short tie at the neck. Leaving her bike by the barn, she walked towards me, a heavy basket on her arm. The Ukrainian man ran to take it. My explanation that I'd had a puncture didn't make her any happier. 'Well, if you've finished, you'd better go, hadn't you?'

She went into the house and slammed the door. I pushed my bike towards the gate, and heard her shouting the vilest swear words, hardly able to believe, and not wanting to, that they were the worst you could hear. She was answered by a few blockbusting retorts from the Ukrainian man as he tried to get a few words in edgeways. Riding away I thought I wouldn't have his life for a pension, though maybe he wasn't as unhappy as he sounded, with his black eye, bruises, and a woman farmer who cursed like a sailor and wore a collar and tie when she went shopping.

The world was alive, the fields living. If there was a God he had stars in his mouth. Thunderflies itched my forehead. I would never die, unless I was killed after joining up. Life was endless. I liked the high wall in front, never wanting to know what was beyond. Backwards or forwards, I didn't care what I was going into. The sky's the limit, I shouted to the sheep, as long as I don't stop moving. Without such a wall I couldn't have lived. Who wanted to know what would happen in a week, a month, a year – even in ten years? More than ever, in ten years. To imagine was one thing, but to know was murder, to which even speculation was getting close.

But I knew that my pal Albert, who had been too bone idle to come with me, could never be a Kettleby. Albert's face also stared out of the wall in front. 'So did you like it, then?' he asked. 'Did you see Alice Sands? Did you get it *in*? Don't tell me you didn't, because I don't believe you. I'll bet you was fucking like rabbits in a thunderstorm.' Or: 'So you did get it in, did you? Tell me another, you barefaced liar.' He was angry that I had gone on my own. He'd expected that when he couldn't go, I shouldn't have gone, either. Then we would still be pals. But now we weren't even friendly. I could see it all. We'd done each other down, and that was the end. I'd never been good at keeping friends.

The roads out of Ab Kettleby took me almost six hundred feet to Broughton Hill, the last big hump between me and the city I was dead set on getting out of. Beyond a straight mile were the upper and nether millstones of the Broughton villages. I passed a pub called the Golden Fleece, and didn't think Jason and his Argonauts had ever drank there.

Outwards and far below was almost the whole bottom half of page 150, the map I had started from – woods, villages, fields, railways and canals, and the River Trent snaking scoremarks across varying shades of green. Home territory had been crisscrossed by cycle, passed through by train or bus, and flown over a few times from Newton or Syerston airfields in Dominie or Dakota. Roaring engines took me south and veered me west. Eyes flitting between map and ground, I'd noted every pond and crossroads. Land of birth for nearly eighteen years, I knew it better than I knew myself, and now I had to leave so as to know only myself, because that was more important.

Many different routes could be taken over the remaining fifteen miles, half-secret lanes which needed no map to find, but even so, I would pedal the main road to the heart, so as to get there sooner in order sooner to get out again.

I looked around and saw the bloke with the tall bike toiling along. Not having stopped for fish and chips, or to sup a shandy, or to mend a puncture, he had made good time. If I didn't get a move on he would catch me up and babble history or politics or even wisdom if we rode together. I didn't want to be bored with such things while riding my bike. If we had been sitting in a pub or hostel common-room it might have been different.

The view from Broughton Hill was the best I could remember, neither too clear nor too hazy, but just soft enough to pull me in. I hadn't even had a better aspect from the air. There would be many other pictures, I told myself as I pumped up the tyres, the back one still not as firm as it should be.

I couldn't stand the sight of the scene, wonderful as it was. I didn't want to go down. To let myself forward with brakes wide open was an unpleasant prospect. The air smelled cold. But I couldn't go back to Stafford, though I worked out a route via Loughborough, Ashby and Burton. Too many memories pushed from behind. I had too much to remember, and couldn't go back. You had to go forward to have more and more to remember, because you never had enough.

Greedy for memories, I had to go on. The past would wither away if I stopped, or ever went backwards. Yet to go forward felt impossible at that moment, though with the man on the tank-bike gaining on me I knew I must set the three-speed, and go downhill as if on Seafire wings, go through what I knew, to get to what I didn't, hoping that pressing on regardless wouldn't always be so painful.

III

I never heard of Oswestry again, which was not surprising. Nor did I make contact with Sheffield and his mates, or ever go back to see the woman at Blatherdene. When I got home there was a letter from the hospital to say that my X-ray plate showed no TB. Another letter said that I had been accepted for the job as an air traffic control assistant, and that I was to go on a short course to an RAF airfield in Buckinghamshire.

I asked my mother where the other letter was.

'What other letter? There's only them two.'

'But there was another,' I said. 'There was three.'

She laughed. 'Don't ask *me*. I only saw two. There couldn't have been three.' But I knew she was lying. 'Your father picks up the letters from the front room mat when he comes down in the morning,' she said. 'We get letters once in a blue moon.'

She looked at me across the table, unwilling, or not able, to tell me that he had ripped it up, and I wanted to burst into tears for her so that I wouldn't have to do it for myself.

PART TWO

I

Morton sat on the terrace of the Unicorn Hotel at Gunthorpe, reflecting on how the road into the future was wide, while the way back was a footpath, mostly unmarked. At eight-thirty on an evening at the end of July the air was full of gnats. A courting couple wandered up-river, a large brown dog reconnoitring in front. The placid landscape was such as only that part of the shallow Trent Valley can lay out for the delectation of someone who grew up there but hadn't been back for years.

Traffic flowed uninterruptedly over the long concrete bridge, on one lane heading south as if to meet the world, and on the other coming back north with equal alacrity to get away from it. The sun was naked above the line of trees. Swifts, tilting over the water but not moving with it, no doubt saw into the depths. A youth for whom the north-south traffic had no relevance cycled along the minor road below.

Under a wide span of the bridge police frogmen were looking for clues on the latest murder. A naked woman bound in chains and weighted with bags of bricks was discovered at that spot two days before. Both the newspaper and the local radio said that the body was bedecked with jewellery to the value of seven hundred pounds. The husband had come from another county, and dropped her, still living, off what he assumed to be a small bridge over an obscure river. He must have been surprised when the police knocked on his bungalow door and said they had found the body. Perhaps he had known all along what he was doing. Paul speculated that two forces were involved inside every person, one being a conscience, which sooner or later betrays that part which commits the evil action. At least he hoped so.

He took a Jamaican cigar out of its tube and touched the delicious leaf with a lighted match. It seemed as if he had lived the past as a somnambulist, yet everything must have been at least as vivid as life was at the moment. He knew more now, though not much. Thirty-eight years since his cycle ride in 1945 was almost the time difference between the Battle of the Somme and Suez. The Israelites had taken forty years to reach the Promised Land. Countless people whose thoughts had enriched the world had died before they had shared the air of the living for that amount of time.

Such a gap had little meaning unless meshed by events related to each other. A single person had but tenuous connections with the past. Only a whole country can make history, millions of people told by television and newspapers – and eventually their own cosy history books – what to remember from the past.

A black vast-winged Vulcan bomber flew above the river, a shadow pushing against the current, flowing over the bridge and out of sight, such noise that everyone looked up from drinking beer or locking their car doors down on the car park. He wished he was in it, for the speed and the view.

The cyclist rode by again. Paul's memory brought things close enough to prove his own cycle ride to be little except a splinter of remembered fact. He couldn't have done anything more sensible than enjoy a week from the factory, but such an action was soon forgotten since it had brought no trouble. Perhaps he recalled his trip because recollections flowered vividly before a change in life, and as for what is trawled back, who is able to single out that event which set you on the track to where you are now?

A few days ago he had injured himself while sawing dead branches from a tree outside his country house. His wife had just left him. It was his third separation; but they were no longer in love, nor had they been so long together that the agony of walking away rendered them too inert to do so. She'd had good reason to go.

With a curved pruning tool he climbed to the top step of the aluminium ladder and got into the branches. Convenient pegs and rungs drew him on, to dismember limbs so that the tree would not die, and to make kindling for winter fires. Branches splintered down, one after the other.

From the top of the tree he saw that the intervening wheat and sheepland took a shallow dip across a canalized river and a line of pylons, then lifted through coppices and hopgardens to a wooded ridge. The sight of the horizon filled his mind with different pictures so exclusively that on descending, and placing his foot on the flat top of the ladder, he must have gone too near the edge. The distance between that and the ground was covered so quickly that it went unrecorded.

The space was not so short, however, that he didn't get up from the ground full of rage at having been struck a powerful blow. The ladder apparently reached earth before him, and he fell across it. Otherwise he might have bounced, been merely bruised and winded. On the other hand maybe the ladder cushioned his fall and stopped him breaking an arm or leg. There was no saying. Whatever thought had imprisoned his faculties to the exclusion of all caution wasn't there by the time he picked himself up, clutching a couple of cracked ribs and cursing as if that alone would bring his breath back. He didn't realize that he had also hurt his wrist, which in the bigger slam went unnoticed.

The local hospital said there was nothing to be done. He would mend in a week or so. Grateful for their lack of fuss he went home and drank a few glasses of whisky, convinced that there could be no better medicine. At night it was impossible to lie still and get to sleep, but if alcohol was a short-term solution, the kill-or-cure attitude of time was another – and more effective.

Life went on. No matter how ill or damaged, or even near death, one would be able to manage the steering wheel of a car. Responsibility for the safety of others, and then for yourself, as well as the drill of accurate driving, would divert the nature of your malady and keep discomfort at bay. So he imagined, and so it turned out. Perhaps cracked ribs weren't serious enough to deter, but it was a start, especially with such difficulties as fastening the seat belt and turning the body to look left and right and to the rear. He did not put off his planned trip to the Midlands. If the thought in his mind at the moment of falling from the tree had been concerned with precisely that area beyond the horizon, and the accident happened in order to put him off the visit, he was even more determined to make it.

II

He stayed the night with his mother and father, as he was obliged to do. It was hard to spend longer with them, however. Both were eighty but healthy, and loved each other as if they were going to live forever. The old man dug his garden, and his mother knitted sweaters. They listened to Radio Nottingham or went to the pub. They smoked countless fags, drank tea continually, and watched television. They talked little because everything had already been said. A laugh was worth a hundred words. A quick look took care of profound comment. A grunt of disapproval that flavoured their opinion of some programme or other would, Paul thought, have needed pages to disentangle. They understood each other too well to need words. After an hour he was threatened with raving madness.

The well-worn council house from the early thirties was just on the homely side of untidiness. Paul's brother, sniffing something rotten in the family, had been in New Zealand for twenty years, and gave no indication of coming back. Paul was their only visitor. He sank into one of two heavy armchairs. As Bismarck had suggested drowning treaties in ink, his parents virtually swamped him during the visit in dose after dose of strong tea. He was given a mug of it to go to bed with, and opened his eyes in the morning to see one approaching broadside on in his father's bony nicotined fist.

Their memories seemed perfect, but whenever Paul mentioned his Uncle Fred they didn't know who he was talking about. They were happy to see him, and unashamedly glad when he left. They had at one time been two islands, but were now joined by a peninsula created when the Seas of Acrimony fell away, leaving a solid neck of land that only a great earthquake could destroy. Nevertheless, they had a sense of humour, and joked about getting a divorce whenever they saw him. They also insisted on filling a two-litre flask with tea when he left.

III

After hours of aimless driving around the city and its outskirts he set off for Edwinstowe. Beyond the village cars lined the verges of Sherwood Forest, where kids and parents were picnicking and playing games. For them the world was static, and the centre of the universe. The sun might bless with warmth, or storm clouds spoil their enjoyment, but they knew who they were because they knew what they wanted.

He turned along a track till the green car was all but invisible from any direction. He opened the four doors and tailgate, lay on his right side and tried to sleep. It took time for the pain to settle, and then he had no dreams. His mind vanished, and so did his body. Where they went he would never know.

When he awoke, the sun shone on birch leaves, and he heard the fluting nostalgic call of the cuckoo over and over again from a deeper part of the forest. He wanted to stay forever, but lay half an hour before standing up. His side burned as if a fire had been lit there. The pain diminished, and he filled a kettle from a container of water, heated it on a small stove, and sat on a fallen trunk to drink his coffee. There was sufficient equipment in the car for a long stay but he felt, as always, that if he wasn't moving he wasn't living.

Driving towards Nottingham, he marvelled at how in an hour he could cover as much distance as he had in a day when cycling at the age of seventeen. A sign outside the Robin Hood restaurant said that a cup of tea at the bar cost fifteen pence. He went south through the rush hour, threading the web of traffic with a panache that he achieved in no other city. The planners had made it easy, but he knew the routes, parallels, roundabouts and one-way systems; streets along which as a youth he would never have imagined himself driving a car.

He stayed that night with Larry Ragnal and his wife Mary, in their opulent new house beyond the river. Larry was a retired wing commander in his middle fifties, much of his lifetime service spent as an air navigator. He was a man still in his prime, intelligent and generous, and as tolerant as anyone can be who has sufficient character to keep his complications in order while realizing that such a feat may not be easy for others.

Paul felt himself so far outside such a state that he had no memory of having been close to it. Tolerance and control should go hand in hand for a man of his age, but zest had turned into greed, and love a sterile pursuit of the unattainable. He reflected that a search for perfection in self and craft carried one across very stony landscapes. Talking to Larry, who had taken over Paul's job in air traffic control when he left to join up, such anxieties were shed away. They recalled that a triangle of three runways was seen from the greenhouse windows of the control tower. A narrow table went around the inside, on which were the switches of the radio telephone gear and weather charts. Larry had gone later as a regular, and though their ways diverged, they retained a common feeling for the occupation they had shared.

A coloured button-map of runways was set out on a panel so that perimeter track and dispersal points could, at the click of a switch, be lit up prettily on map and ground at the same time, when evening came prematurely and a plane was due to arrive. Log books, pencils, plotting charts, telephones and cups were scattered around. On a corner table a hotplate for making tea and toasting bread gave off a homely smell on afternoons when cold mist hung at the windows during Paul's long winter. The flying control officer, a grey-haired squadron leader of forty, whom the assistants referred to among themselves as 'Pop', mused over the *Daily Telegraph* crossword, while Paul worked out square-search or interception problems on a Dalton computer, or played darts with the other air traffic control assistant. Real life had begun, as if he had never worked in a factory.

Across the road were A.V. Roe hangars where York airliners were assembled. The test pilot took Paul up over the city and environs, though without signing his cadet log book because he was not supposed to be on board. That winter the Trent had overflowed into the streets. From the cockpit of the large aeroplane, empty but for the two of them, he saw the devastation of water, the misery of a cold flood deep into every house. On the way back he settled himself at the ample navigation table and imagined he had been asked to plot a series of courses to Australia.

Each morning when flying was to take place he would set out the white planks in the signals square by the tower to make a 'T', to indicate the current wind for landing. From the turret of the black-and-white checkerboard caravan at the beginning of the runway, where a similar 'T' had been laid out on the grass by its side, he would be ready to signal incoming aircraft with a green flash from the Aldis lamp if the runway was clear, and red if it was not. He laughed at the idea of being a human traffic light so early on in life.

On control tower duty he would sometimes go onto the perimeter track to guide an aircraft to a dispersal point, walking backwards with two coloured handbats, the oncoming engines of an Avro Anson moving slowly forward, while Paul prayed he would not stumble and make a fool of himself. When the plane wanted to leave he would pull away the chocks and climb onto the wing with a starting handle to prime the engines before take off.

Because he lived only twelve miles away he didn't qualify for a billet in the village. If he had, life would have been perfect. He had applied for the job hoping that would be the case. But he got up at six o'clock in the morning and from the city centre caught a second bus, with other aircraft workers, to the aerodrome, a view of frosty fields from the smoke-filled top deck while he read every word of the *Daily Herald*.

When he arrived at half past seven the first thing to do at the tower was make tea, and take a pot down to the air traffic control officer who slept below and was still in bed. Back upstairs he tuned in the wireless for weather reports from airfields around Great Britain and plotted them on a chart. He phoned neighbouring airfields to get the weather locally, at first hardly able to hold his pencil on hearing a WAAF reciting figures in a more attractive voice than Edith Weston's could possibly be.

When the other assistant arrived from his digs in the village one of them would, according to the roster, walk along the perimeter track to the caravan at the end of the runway, though if the wind had changed in the night (he would glance at the windsock while walking from the bus) they would phone for a tractor to pull it to another position.

At seventeen the sense of power was inebriating. The responsibility cleared his head. He spoke into wireless and telephone with as little accent as possible. Even more than in the factory, or in the cadets while on the firing range, rules and regulations concerned the safety of life.

Most incoming aeroplanes announced their imminence through the RAF exchange in a room below. A fire tender and blood wagon would then be standing by. When a kite joined the circuit without warning the assistant in the caravan called the tower by field telephone and tried to delay flashing a green light to say that the runway was clear until the ambulance and fire tender had been contacted.

Boiling a kettle on the caravan stove, he heard a plane fly low and settle itself on the runway. From the turret he should have warned it off till safety arrangements had been made, or at least have noted its number and time of landing in the log book. Cloud was five thousand feet at two-tenths, so there was no excuse. No one was aware in the tower. No fire tender or blood wagon was waiting. It was Paul's fault entirely, the worse thing that could have happened. If the plane had crashed the crew would have been lost for want of immediate assistance. The first rule in the book had been broken. The squadron leader tore him off a hundred strips. Maybe he would have been dismissed if the tea he made in the morning hadn't been so good. But an even bigger strip was torn off the pilot.

Recollections at Larry Ragnal's took place over good whisky and a box of powerful cigars, and it was two in the morning before they had talked themselves dry. Paul's life at the control tower was more vivid than the cycle ride, but only because it had lasted forty times as long.

IV

After an early start he headed towards Stafford. It was the same time of the year. Sheltered in his mobile tin, fearing no bad weather, the two thousand cubic centimetres of engine capacity allowed him to scoot without effort along the route he had once cycled. There was no sweat of pedalling, only the mental energy of avoiding danger on the road. Bolstered in every sense, insured for all contingencies, he had more cash in his wallet than the seventeen-year-old could have earned in a couple of months. He also had chequebooks, credit cards, and travellers' cheques from his last journey to New York. Half a dozen shirts and a change of clothes made him self-sufficient: the only person more secure, he thought, would be a factory worker who lived at home, but how safe was he when redundancy could come almost without notice?

From the indifferent atlas carried at seventeen he had sheets of metric maps for the whole route. A cardboard box overflowed with Michelin, AA, RAC, Postgate, Baedeker, Good Hotel and Blue Guide books, some of them out of date. Even so, having passed the Blue Ball at Risley, he lost the old road into Derby and strayed onto the dual carriageway. Maps were next to useless if you had no navigator. He did the rounds twice, channelled through soulless one-way streets, side glances indicating that the town's middle had been blitzed even more than usual by the 'planners'.

Sweating, he lowered a window. The country landscape had altered less. Houses on the road to Uttoxeter had aged, though paint and repairs made some look better. Contact with his former self seemed almost nil. Other people came back more vividly. What had happened to the youth who had cycled with him as far as Uttoxeter? Was he contented with his wife, children, and perhaps grandchildren? Had he made it up with his father and gone into his profession? If his parents still lived they were no doubt shamelessly happy at the General Election of a few days ago, when the Tory landslide was a result almost as good, or as bad, as the Labour victory in 1945. If Oswestry had by any chance seen Paul's films on television he wouldn't have realized they had been written by him, because they had not exchanged names.

Driving round a bend he stopped and walked back to a bridge, the wind warm at his clean-shaven face. The surface of the sluggish brook was covered in scum. Like my memory, he said to himself. I can't get through without parting the green slime. He stared, didn't even drop a stone into it.

After 'The High Noon Rest Home' the road was straight, fields on either side. Blue election pennants were nailed on trees as if to indicate the way to some barbaric spectacle. Mrs Thatcher was back, and no one would be able to make any mistake about that. A cyclist bent against the wind came along the unchanging bucolic uplands.

He stopped at the same place in Uttoxeter. The woman who served his coffee seemed a replica of the one before. She called him duck on asking if he wanted anything to eat, and though identical metal lamps hung from the ceiling, no spinal tug made him cry out in recognition.

He took off his jacket before getting into the hot car. The only habit which betrayed his class origins – if there was such a thing – was that when with other people at a concert or party he liked to wear a suit instead of jeans, sweatshirt, sneakers and, maybe, a beard. Some of his one-time middle-class left-wing friends couldn't forgive him for persisting in being, he thought, more working class in this respect than they would ever know how to be.

He drove out of town and over the level crossing, then up a hill barely noticed in his large Volvo. Woods and fields, woods and fields. He must have got tired on that long pull to Stafford, a never-ending uphill-and-down on a handful of bread and cheese, though he remembered how his encounter with the man on the horse had powered the dynamo. Whatever the horseman's motive, perhaps there was something to thank him for.

He felt different because he was older. Otherwise he was the same, a fish in water like everyone else. The revolution had come and gone, a pimple on the social landscape which got flatter as time went by. The long wall at Loxley on which he had leaned his bike seemed to go along the side of the road forever. Ivy and elderberry bushes had pulled it to pieces since he rode that way. Nettles sprouted from the rubble. Sections were crumbling, but only in places far enough apart to maintain the illusion that what it protected would always stay intact. Even the Great Wall of China had not held out change. More Victory posters fastened to the trees testified to Labour's devastation.

The man on the horse would have his day for a long time to come, unless the dogs of civil war tore him from his perch. If by any chance such a calamity did occur, the man in the tank, with a cigar in his mouth and a beret on his head (or the British equivalent) would take his place, and make things so bad that present conditions would be looked back on as paradise by everyone without exception. How many of his friends of the sixties had thought that such a person as Che Guevara would be their salvation? Paul had long since taken the classic poster down, and thrown *The Little Red Book* into the dustbin. When some of the Left had come out on the side of anti-semitism he knew he had had enough.

He put down the shade to prevent the sun's dazzle,

which cut out part of the green landscape. In Stafford, while trying to find the Temperance Hotel where he had stayed in 1945, he recognized nothing. One-way streets and pedestrian areas were flanked by raw-bricked stores. People loved the glitter and newness, and the convenience. He supposed the hotel no longer existed. The navvies who had offered him work were old or dead.

Car parks were full, so he drove to the aerodrome where he had met Alice Sands, though he knew for sure he would not see her now. He had the address of the house she had lived in, but couldn't drum up the guts to call. She was a farmer's wife with stern look, glinting glasses, grey hair, and a husband to match, worn out by work and the rearing of four children who had left home. Women's Liberation hadn't reached this far, and if it had she was too old to benefit.

She wouldn't even remember.

'Who?' her husband standing behind would ask. 'An old boyfriend? I'll kill him. Here, where's my shotgun? No, ask him in for a cup of tea. Let's see what he's made of.'

They might imagine he was trying to sell something, or wanted to buy their antiques for next to nothing.

'Tell him he's come to the wrong house, Alice, unless he wants to cart *us* away. And for God's sake, get my dinner on the table. I'm bloody starving.'

The aerodrome would mark the landscape for a hundred years. Holed and cobbled runways were too expensive to eradicate. Flocks of Oxford Trainers on circuits-and-bumps were things of memory. But he heard the sound of their engines, smelled upholstery and high-octane fuel, and the odour of captive stale sunlight when opening the door of an aircraft to clamber in with a parachute hanging under his arse, and trying to keep his cap on for fear of being thought disrespectful to the pilots. He felt himself separating from the fields and hedges and patches of wood as the plane gained height and headed towards the ruined crenellations of Wishdale Abbey.

The control tower, similar to the one he and Larry Ragnal had worked at, was boarded up. Black hangars had been turned into a warehouse-depot across the road. A couple of juggernaut lorries headed towards Stafford and the M6, London three hours away when it used to be more than five.

Trees and bushes were the same. He stopped the car and got out to look at the airfield. Pulling a leaf from the hedge he squeezed it between his fingers till juice came, an odour which took him back even further than the age of seventeen.

The farmhand wound down his window to see if Paul needed help. 'Oh yes, we get a lot of these air force chaps coming back to look at the aerodrome. They try and get into it, poor old souls, but fall into the ditch as often as not. We have to pick 'em out of the brambles. Oh, they just come to have a look. People are funny that way. Can't understand it myself.'

He drove off, disappointed that Paul wasn't old enough to repeat an act which would be as funny as anything he could record on his video machine.

Stafford was crowded. He stopped himself looking intently into every face in the hope of seeing Alice Sands. He searched instead for a place to eat, and in a remnant of the old town found a chop house called Cambers. The large low room was almost full for dinner – as he would have called it in the old days. The waitress sat him facing a bald and portly man of sixty who, in such stifling weather, wore tie and jacket and waistcoat. He might have been a magistrate's clerk, and

187

looked slightly miserable, though not from being overdressed. His face bore the pained expression of the bachelor, rather than the tightened anguish of the husband.

Paul tried to recall the meals eaten during his former time in Stafford. His dinner in the British Restaurant at Coventry was nothing as elaborate as this archetypal English feed of rich soup; roast beef, Yorkshire pudding, potatoes and three kinds of vegetables; apple pie and custard. He finished with a cup of coffee, and only the Caribbean cigar was good. The soup suggested melted dripping and gravy powder. The roast beef was like sheets of brown paper. The Yorkshire pudding was flat and hard. The vegetables were overcooked. The dessert had no taste. Something was lacking, and it wasn't only the uncritical hunger of youth. Even at seventeen he would have known how unpretentiously rotten it was.

The man consumed his cottage pie. His distinctive features were close together and well-centred in the middle of his rather obese face. At Paul's smile he mentioned how good the meal tasted. His grey eyes were beyond rumination, but not unfriendly. 'I eat here every day. There aren't many places where you get a proper businessman's lunch.' They spoke about the weather. Paul told him he was passing through Stafford. 'You were lucky to find this place to eat at, then.'

Paul agreed. He never argued when he wanted information. 'I stumbled on it by accident. I haven't been here since 1945. The town's altered a fair bit since then.'

'It certainly has. It's changed absolutely since I came here from Stoke twenty years ago. It used to be a much better place.'

Paul hoped the man could have told him about the town at the time of his cycle trip. He probed, but got nothing useful. He may have been interested in what Paul did for a living, but was too diffident to ask. When anyone did, he said he was a bookseller. Nor would Paul question him, thinking it better to concoct the details of an existence which might have been more useful than his own, and hardly less interesting. What he didn't known about the town he would have to make up, and be satisfied. He had, after all, spent his life creating reality out of lies, so it should not be hard.

V

He parked as far into the hedge as possible so as not to cause an obstruction. On the other hand he didn't want to scratch his car, or sink a wheel into the mud so that it would need a tractor to pull him out, which he supposed had happened more to him than anyone else.

It was obvious, opening the gate-latch and going down the path, that the building was two cottages. One stood at right-angles to the other, darkening red bricks giving a worn appearance to the walls. The roof was of plain slate. Across a space of cinderpath and black soil were a few decrepit sheds. By the side of the building the body of a yellow and blue motor car rotted away.

The garden behind looked as well cultivated as that in front. Paul stood under the wooden awning by the open door, hearing the plangent hectoring of a male television voice from inside the house. He hoped that nobody would answer his knock, and thought that after counting silently to ten he would make off. But he heedlessly embarked on a second ten, and before reaching the end an old man came to see what he wanted.

The area was a network of lanes, with few houses

except those in the village. Repair signs were up on one stretch where no workmen were, but they slowed him down so that, round a bend and up a slight rise, he had seen the house divided from the road by a short zone of garden. He had no option but to call.

Frail in the face, the old man's vigour was obvious when a dog like a giant earwig tried to push between his legs and was repelled by the thrust of a well-laced boot. He looked at Paul through black spectacles, a hint of water in brown eyes. Seventy-five, if he's a day. The long, broad-bladed knife in his left hand showed he had not been idle while seated at the television set. Maybe doing some craftwork which did not call for much finesse. Paul regretted having pulled him from his entertainment, but the man did not seem to mind.

'What do you want, then?'

The smell of chrysanthemums, roses, and Staffordshire soil carried a plump bee across his nose and in a panic out through the porch. 'I was at the aerodrome once, near the end of the war, and I knew a girl called Alice Sands. I wondered if she was still in the neighbourhood.'

It was a long jump to go so far back. He took the big curved pipe out of his mouth, and Paul thought his teeth would come away with it. His own might have. 'They don't live here anymore.'

He hadn't expected them to. 'I'm sorry about that.'

The old man looked as if Paul was as barmy as he, in his lucid moments, felt himself fast becoming. 'Haven't lived here in a long time.'

'I just wondered.'

A glitter shot across both eyes. Or it might have been the sun on his glasses. 'I was in the Forces in them days.' He straightened. 'Oh yes, I was a drill instructor, training the lads for the North Staffordshire Regiment.'

Paul hoped he wouldn't maunder off into a short history of the Second World War, which would take a couple of hours, a habit more of them developed the further away it got. 'Is that so?'

'I remember Mr Sands, all right. A bit of a runagate, old Jerry was. Well, both of us were, if you want to know the truth. Who wasn't in them days?' He winked, and laughed, and coughed, and resisted scratching himself, and Paul stepped aside in case he should think to nudge him with the sharp end of the knife. He arranged the spectacles back on the bridge of his nose. 'He died ten years ago. His wife Ada settled down in Devon, with her sister. I expect she's gone now. Everybody has. Or they're going.' He didn't seem particularly sorry about it, or worry that he too would one day 'go'.

Neither did Paul want a rundown on family and kinship in the West Midlands, whether or not the old man relished a stint away from the television set – though he couldn't fault him for that. 'Devon's a fine place,' he said, so as to get him going again.

'Maybe, but not half as pretty as Staffordshire. Mind you, I'd go down to Devon myself if I could afford it. Or if I had relations there. Don't suppose they'd like it, though, if I did.'

'So Alice went with her mother?' He imagined speeding along sunken lanes on the edge of Dartmoor to look for her in the morning. Get onto the M5, and he would be there in a few hours, after picking up a meal in his Somerset cottage.

The knife went up and down the old man's thighs as if cutting away cobwebs. 'No, not our Alice, she didn't. I was demobbed in forty-six, you see, just in time for her wedding. We hadn't seen such a wedding around here for a long time, not since 1938 when Lord Bend's

191

daughter got spliced from Tadpole Hall, over yonder. Alice got hooked to a Canadian, an air force chap, an officer he was. His folks came over from Canada, and that took some doing, just after the war. But they could afford it, and I reckon they enjoyed themselves. They had some family here, anyway, in Scotland. Then Alice went off with them to Toronto. Her husband's a lawyer, a fine feller.'

'I'm glad to hear that.'

'They came back last year. Stayed at the Grand Hotel in Birmingham, and drove out to see the old place. She must be fifty, but don't look nowhere near it. You'd tek her for thirty, if you didn't know who she was. He's worn a bit, poor chap. Got a bad heart. Alice don't alter, though. She looked like that lovely young thing on television – what's her name? – oh, I had it a minute ago.' He held Paul's lapel. 'Do you know, I remember Alice when she was a little gel? She used to run out of the back door to chase the chickens. What a terror! She was a lovely little kid. Oh, I know who it was now. She's the spitten-image of that smashing young Muriel Fletcher on the telly, the one as got married the other day. Do you remember?'

When Paul indicated that he did not, the old man thought it time he started to live and find out what life was all about. 'Everybody knows her. But she's wasted on that playboy she got hitched to, I'll tell you that much. I can never understand why lovely gels go out with such bloody rotters. Can you tell me? You can see he's rotten through and through.'

Paul nodded, half afraid of such vindictiveness, and wondered whether he could stop him before he ran out of energy. Yet the old man was so animated he looked twenty years younger.

'Anybody with half an eye can see what he's like.

He's going to lead her a dance right enough, with his blond hair and pretty blue eyes. A jiggerlow if ever I saw one. No way would I have married him if I'd been her. No damned way at all!'

He didn't know how right he was.

'It's enough to break your heart, in't it? Bloody rotten to the core he is.'

Paul didn't say that he had written the scripts for two of Muriel Fletcher's films. If the old man thought he was in some way responsible for her marital disaster he might ply a bit more decisively with the knife. But if he could still wield it for that purpose, it wouldn't be for much longer. Nor would Paul tell him that only a few weeks ago he had been driving with the delectable Muriel Fletcher at a hundred miles an hour along the M4 at midnight because she'd had a phone call from her teenaged drug-addicted daughter who had screamed down the line that she was going to kill herself. The crazy bitch had already rung Paul's wife to say who he was with. Next day his wife had walked out, and was now threatening him with his third divorce.

'Did Alice have any children?'

'Eh? What? Oh yes, she did.' He was brought down to earth, if it could be called that, and he didn't like it. 'She had a couple. Grown up and gone away by now. They all do. She had the first just after they got married. A little boy.'

He wanted to get back to reality on the television, but Paul put a final question. 'She had a mate called Gwen. What happened to her?'

He didn't have to think. 'Oh, her? Married a farmer's lad up near Eccleshall. Never see her. But Alice, she's a lovely woman. Allus was. Just like that Muriel Fletcher.'

Television had blunted his life by making him a slave

to it, but at least he had connected the shape of Muriel Fletcher's mouth with that of Alice Sands's. Paul couldn't fault him for that. Muriel Fletcher, however, did not have the same shapeless nose as Alice.

VI

He got his tank filled for twenty quid, water put in the radiator, oil topped up. Questions he hadn't thought of came during the drive to Stafford Castle. A tape played 'Plaisirs d'Amour' by Giovanni Martini, but he pushed it off halfway through.

The needle clocked fifty. No one has any control over the grand design, he supposed. Answers come only, if at all, at their leisure. We make our pictures and slot them into place. Other people witness them on television screens, which rob them of their lives. The poor are those who watch television, whatever income they have.

He stayed in the car and, by a notice saying NO VEHICLES BEYOND THIS POINT rewound the tape to hear the whole of Martini's melancholy song. The gravel track was wide enough to drive on, but he threw down his cigar and set off to walk. He was soon panting at the slope, every inhalation a pain in the ribs. He wondered whether the fall hadn't injured his lung. The doctor had merely prodded his side as if trying to see whether he could make him faint. Old Loewenthal would have known better. A full breath was impossible. He couldn't yawn or cough. To sneeze was a catastrophe. However funny something seemed, laughter was blocked.

He walked on, till he recognized the stark fortress against the sky. A score of archaeologists worked at various diggings. What pots or bones or weapons would

they find? One group had a transistor radio, but much
of its tinkling was drowned by motorway noise, and the
bumping of the wind. A patch had been cut out of the
tree zone to give the Castle a wide field of fire. He went
back to the car, a hand pressing on his wound.

VII

The magpie danced, and lifted off. He drove through
lanes to the place where he first met Alice. What part of
the hedge was impossible to say. His past had been
thieved by time, separated from his consciousness like
oil from water, and buried out of sight, no Ben Gunn as
on Treasure Island to keep it safe. Trees were evenly
spaced, sheep grazing between, looking like white
plasticine under painted lead models. He walked from
the road, into the wind. Across the fields, woods hid the
Abbey. Crows cawed above the rattle of tree branches.
A bullock looked at him with pale blue eyes, as if he
could save it from slaughtertime. He couldn't even save
himself.

Black and white cows lay in the second field. He had
unthinkingly found beautiful places in those days. If
such a board had existed in that ration-book utility era
it had been a little less wordy than PRIVATE
PROPERTY KEEP OUT TRESPASSERS WILL BE PROSE-
CUTED BY ORDER OF THE TRUSTEES OF THE WISHDALE
ABBEY ESTATE. He and Albert would have wandered in
regardless. Peewits flew over half-cut grass. He hadn't
seen Albert since then. Rhododendrons made
a purple gash on the hillside.

Another warning close to the grounds should, he
thought, have a gamekeeper's deerstalker hat on top.
Looking through binoculars, he saw trees growing from

the building, though some walls were in a fair state of brickwork, mortar neat between the gaps. The glasses back in their case, he hesitated as a trespasser at further intimidating boards.

Enormous rose bushes had given way to a proliferation of nettles. Rubble and the green tentacles of vegetation defended the exterior of the building. He remembered stepping high along the charred beams, and balancing as if showing off to the girls who dared not look – except that they hadn't been there.

The footholds felt just as solid. He was twenty feet from the ground. There was a hole in his consciousness, a vacuum blocking off thought and air with such completeness that he was frightened. The same lapse had taken place before falling from the tree. Trembling, he let himself down. It would be suicide to climb as high as before, or a test of nerve, or an acknowledgement of the years that had gone by. For what better purpose could he break his neck?

He touched the slippery stairs with respect, the skin as cold as a toad's, and stayed close to the wall. He did not need proof of his nerve. This height would supply that. He could write about the rest. His imagination had not so far let him down.

Uncle Fred told him to come up and join the Club. 'There's nothing to it. You'll never forget the view.'

'I've seen it already.'

'You were too young to appreciate it.'

Working in the factory had started him with hardened muscles. Rowing and swimming kept them strong. But if he came loose and grabbed a protruding stump his cracked ribs would weaken him. Unable to latch on at the moment of collapse, he would be beyond help.

He was surprised at how easy it was. Fred did not

need to beckon. The picture of him as an active and rational man came back from childhood, and cleared Paul's brain of any stricture for being such a fool. 'It's the survival of the fittest,' Fred taunted. 'How can you live without coming up? You'll never regret it.'

Timbers had been replaced in a hotchpotch attempt at restoration. Some were more rotten than before. 'I thought you were my friend!'

Fred laughed.

There was nothing to lose. The climb became a pleasure. The suicidal urge was a small price to pay for feeling young. He surveyed the countryside from the topmost rafter. Airspeed Oxfords with their course-pilots did not take off anymore from the aerodrome. To avoid the strong wind he held himself against a piece of wall, while he picked off a chunk of slate and put it in his pocket. He let another slice fall. Bushes cushioned the smash. He looked for his initials but couldn't find them. He had let go of the ground so as to say goodbye to Alice, and farewell to the bike ride that had brought him back. Memory is a gift. It gives a meaning to life that no one can take away, Fred informed him.

The ruinous structure below was encased in a filigree zone of ivy. He did not want to go down. When he was alone in the kitchen with Uncle Fred he switched on the radio and heard an opera coming direct from Italy. Fred turned up the volume and told him to listen. Sun shone but he had put on the electric light. The applause was as thrilling as if the performance was taking place in the room.

Fred lay back in the armchair. 'I was in Italy once,' he said. 'A wonderful country.'

He came and went, Paul had heard his father say about Fred. His eyeballs spun, and then they died – and spun again. Maybe he always did that when such music played on the wireless. It was an old trick of his. Paul wasn't afraid. He didn't know what an opera was, but sat at the table with his meal going cold.

Fred moved his hand in time to a grand all-sweeping tune that seemed to fill the house and even the sky outside. His parents had gone to see doctors about having Fred put into an asylum, and Paul thought maybe they had gone together, and left them alone, in the hope that Fred would have one of his awful fits and murder him, so that they could be rid of both at the same time. They didn't realize that all they had to do was wait a few years.

Tears slopped onto his Uncle Fred's waistcoat. Entranced by the music of *Tosca* from Milan, Paul had the conviction that Fred was his real father, and not the man who was out with his mother.

'It's taken you a damned long time to tumble to it,' Fred told him when they stood together on the topmost tower of Wishdale Abbey. 'People were a bit sharper in my day than they seem to be in yours. But don't let it worry you. When that funny business was going on between me and your parents we were only in our thirties – nearly twenty years younger than you are now. What do you think of that, then? If I were you I'd get down from here as fast as you can, before the funniest thing happens of all.'

When he last stayed in Milan the Italian film producer Mario Salvatore took him to hear *Tosca* at La Scala.

VIII

He drove over the river, and then the canal. A jogger was working his way back into Stafford. Nobody ran in his day. With so few buses they had to bike or walk, and that was sufficient exercise. Enough had changed to make a man feel a stranger in the land by the time he got to middle age.

Alice wrote neatly on small lined pages. He regretted not keeping her letters. There must have been three or four. He had nothing from those days. As soon as he joined up his books and papers had been thrown away. His clothes were given to the ragman, the bicycle sold. He never knew why. His mother said that his father had done it. Paul reminded him too much of his Uncle Fred, and so did his belongings, which were got rid of even more ruthlessly than Fred's. Yet he himself, before joining up, had put schoolbooks and papers in the dustbin, Alice's letters among them. He couldn't bear possessions, those tentpegs of memory. So memory took its revenge.

The presence of her letters came back as if he could reach out and touch them. He opened the glove box to make sure they were not there. He tapped his pockets, expecting to hear a crinkle of paper. They had been thrown away during a state of oblivion similar to that which had caused him to pitch headlong from the tree whose existence he had been trying to prolong. His faculties were blotted out, and allowed him no say in what profoundly mattered. To lose control filled him with dismay. To commit actions which he had never intended, and have moments pass whose thoughts he couldn't recall, made for a fearful existence.

It had taken him a long time to realize that no man was the guide and architect of his life. Nearly forty years in the wilderness should have prepared him for the fact that the most profound decisions were not finally made by him.

Trying to trace where he had slept on the second

night of his bicycle trip, he couldn't decide whether the inn had been before Lichfield or after Lichfield, on the left-hand side of the road, or to the right-hand, before or after Tamworth. It was surely in that region, and even on the left-hand side of the road rather than the right. He drove back and forth, putting his and other lives in peril by performing rapid manoeuvres in awkward places, some of the turns less skilful due to the pain in his ribs brought on by any sudden exertion.

The paper map from Stafford on which he had written dates, names, prices and stopping places had been torn up in a rented house on the northern coast of Sardinia ten years later. Folded and unfolded so many times to work out theoretical military exercises, or to fashion landscapes as a background for stories, the map had all but fallen to pieces, and went towards making a fire on a gloomy Mediterranean afternoon.

The cycle trip for which the map was used had not been in his mind, but he now remembered writing on it. Many was the plot of a script or scrap of dialogue that he had later worked out on the remaining space. These days he kept a small hand-held tape recorder in the glove box for any idea which might improve a piece of work. The only item to survive those days was the handbook of wild flowers which he kept on the shelf of his cottage in Somerset. How either that or the map had escaped his father's clear-out he would never know.

The Feathers, on the left-hand side of the road before Lichfield, didn't look old enough. The backyard was paved, and there was neither garden nor large accommodation hut. A homely pub at Coton, just before Tamworth, seemed to be the right one. Why had he assumed for so many years that his night stop had been before Lichfield? Then he wondered whether it wasn't The Horse and Jockey, just after Lichfield.

There were housing estates on the edge of each town, streets tacked onto the main road, groups of new dwellings which had not been there before. Town centres were different. Main roads round them had been widened and straightened. Bits of the tortuous road had become lay-bys. Trunk routes acquired junction and roundabout systems covering areas as large as the old town centres themselves, thus wiping out features which might have helped to identify specific points.

Some stretches of road were more or less the same, but there was no reason why the pub should be easier to locate than to discover what had happened to the erring granddaughter who had gone off with her lorry driver. Reconnoitring a few miles back and forth proved that the inn before Lichfield had certainly gone. All the schools he had been to, and the house he was born in, had also been destroyed and built over. Planning had done it, not war. He only regretted that memory would not allow him to satisfy his curiosity concerning the inn he had stayed at, but then, even the Israelites had not thought to go back over the forty-year route before accepting their fate in the Promised Land.

The search was relinquished. You attempt to go back when you feel a need to go forward for the last time. The seventeen-year-old youth riding that stretch of road was impossible to bring into the present. How much in fact was me? he wondered. He had become the dead tree, as well as that naïve figure falling from it like one of the firewood branches he had cut off. He had cycled blithely down from Broughton Hill and never come back to himself. He had always wanted to escape, because it was the only way he could stay alive. He had been in tune with that blank spot of his mind, and his own Fate had decided to be his guide.

IX

Nor could he be certain of his route between Lichfield and Coventry. He had passed that twenty-five-mile stretch so intensely preoccupied with the events of the previous forty-eight hours that he noticed nothing. No doubt he had stopped to eat an apple, or turn the page of his atlas as if in a waking dream, his body inseparable from the wheels of the bicycle.

Huts and prefabs in Coventry had been replaced by office blocks and shopping precincts. The place reminded him of reconstructed cities in East Germany which seemed never to catch up with the fact that they had come back to life. He went through in a few minutes, and a man by the main road holding a clipboard made signs of wanting a lift.

In a photoflash Paul registered that he was about forty, wore a conventional jacket and trousers, and a shirt without a tie. He probably belonged to a surveying gang, and wanted to go a few miles down the road. His hair was black, short-back-and-sides, and he pulled the door open without being told.

'Where are you going?'

He hesitated before settling himself in. 'Daventry.'

Paul hoped he wouldn't talk much, so that he could absorb details of his cycle route. The clipboard had been a ploy to inspire passing drivers into giving him a lift. 'Do you live there?'

His face was lined and suntanned, as if he worked in the open air. A glance via the mirror showed that his clothes were worn. There was a slight reek, as if he had slept in them. 'No sir. I'm going to London. I can get onto the M1 from Daventry.'

A car came out of a side road without caution, causing Paul to press on the brake. He made a point of never using the hooter. 'Do you have family there?'

'I'm going to get work.'

'What sort?'

He blew his nose. 'On a building site, if I can. Even as a tea-lad, if they'll have me.' The laugh was not bitter, but an expression of the dispossessed who did not mind being without illusions. It was an English laugh, and all the more human for that. Times change, and the mighty are fallen. Who does he think I am, Paul wondered, graciously giving him a lift in my tin palace? He could kill me, but it wouldn't improve matters, and might well make things worse. 'I'm grateful to you for helping me.'

'Where did you set out from?'

'Liverpool. This morning at six. Motorists don't stop so often these days for chaps like me. I stand at the side of the road, but they don't want to know.'

'Hard to fathom why not.' Paul meant it. 'Doesn't cost anything in petrol to have an extra person in the car.'

'Ah, but they don't all think like that.'

The man didn't want to talk, either. He'd had enough. Too tired, perhaps. Talking never did any good. He would only retreat into his conservation area. Paul didn't want to embarrass him by picking up his tape recorder and speaking notes into it, but a story could be made up, of giving somebody a lift who, after a few moments, points a gun at the driver. The hitchhiker is a terrorist on the run: 'Drive me to Liverpool, or I'll kill you.' But the driver had set out from home that morning determined to commit suicide by driving himself and the car off Beachy Head. He had often decided to do it, and had each time ended up laughing at himself as he drove home with a present for his wife. But on this day he was deadly serious, until the terrorist pointed a gun at him. Then he had a purpose in life. What a story! The driver doesn't mind killing himself by scooting off Beachy Head (a long marvellous shot to show on the screen!) but to be forced into an action he doesn't want to do by this raw-faced hand-trembling gun-carrying shit-head of a tuppenny terrorist was more than he has bargained for.

He stops laughing. 'Liverpool, you said?' But he won't turn the car in that direction, in spite of the terrorist becoming more frantic and threatening: 'I'll kill you!'

'Shoot, then,' says the driver, 'and kill us both.' He smiles: 'Go on, shoot, do me a favour!' He is quite calm about it. They go on for miles, following the Eastbourne signposts. He won't turn the car, and he won't stop. He wants to kill the terrorist, as well as himself. What a bonus! Take one with you! And what an unlucky day for the terrorist, that he picked him and not some mild little bloke in a Morris Minor who would have done what he was told and no messing.

The driver wants to kill the terrorist for assuming that his crazy political notions are more important than his (the driver's) emotional and domestic agony which he had been suffering under for twenty years and from which he is now going to release himself. He wonders whether he should tell the terrorist what he has in mind. He's driving very fast, and the terrorist can only stop him by firing the pistol and killing them both. The terrorist is afraid to die, and our driver is terrorizing the terrorist. It's almost good enough to stay alive for, but it's only so good because he is going to kill himself. The terrorist is being kept hostage, roles reversed.

The driver tells him his intention at last. It's too

good to keep to himself. The terrorist then pleads for his life. The driver says that he can live, but he must throw the gun out of the window. To prove he's serious the driver overtakes a juggernaut on a bend. They escape death by inches. The terrorist is petrified, sits with the gun on his knees. It's a novel situation. The handbooks from South America or Baghdad never dealt with this one.

The terrorist starts spluttering about how he's fighting for his Third World oppressed, colonized, underprivileged people. The bilge of his political credo comes out in fits and starts. He has to talk fast because there are only eleven miles left to Beachy Head. Instead of a grenade in his hand, or one which he is strapping to some victim's chest, he is actually inside a grenade from which the pin has already been pulled.

I'll call the story UNLUCKY DAY, Paul thought.

The terrorist dies again and again. The driver thinks that eleven more miles is too short a distance to complete his purpose. He makes a detour. He could go on all day, all night. He has never felt so active, so alive, so full of life, so little like dying. That will be my mistake, he thinks, intending to get back onto the main road as soon as possible. If I stop wanting to die, the game's over. Yet when the game is over, I'll be dead, and I don't want the game to end. It's the first time in my life I'm really enjoying something. There's a price for everything, and every price finds its own level.

In any case, he can't drive around south-east England forever, or he'll run out of petrol. The tank's half full, just enough to cause a conflagration as he hits the rocks, providing the tide is out – he tells the terrorist, who then thinks it might after all be better if the driver carries on till little petrol is left in the tank. The impact will kill them, anyway. He fastens his safety belt, and the driver doesn't object. You never know. The impact, no matter what the height, might not kill, and to die by fire is the final horror. I suppose my captive terrorist laughed hilariously, the driver ruminates, when he read about eighty people being burnt to death by Arab terrorists raking an airliner with machine guns on the runway and setting it alight. Let him worry, because round and round we go, since I don't want to die by fire either.

Well, of course, the ending is another matter. There's always more than one ending, if a story is to stay anywhere close to real life. Does our driver 'take one with him'? Perhaps, first of all, he reaches for his little tape recorder and speaks into it, telling of how he was hijacked by this terrorist, and bravely decides to die a George Medal death by killing him at the cost of his own life. They are listening to his last words in the police station, taking off their hats and helmets in respectful silence at his final calm cool matter-of-fact British airline pilot's kamikaze words: 'Over and out.' The small tape will survive if there is no fire, so he decides to go on and on until fuel is all but finished.

Another ending is that he goes on so long that the terrorist cracks up and surrenders to him. The driver has only to stop at the first copper's cottage in some village and hand him over. But then he is back to square one. Maybe I should call the story SQUARE ONE, and it ends with our driver getting just enough petrol at a filling station to reach Beachy Head, careful this time not to pick up anyone hitching a lift.

You always get back to square one. The wide horizons of Warwickshire revealed the same clusters of Marconi's cloudscratchers sending messages by radio teletype and tropospheric scatter, or whatever it was, print and pictures bounced from satellites and going to

206

just as many places as there used to be in the British Empire.

He covered in an hour what had taken a day on the bike, floating along the main road towards Daventry with the sound of Handel's *Israel in Egypt* filling the car. He pumped water up the windscreen to clean off the juice of gnats, the wipers beating time to the kind of music which showed how far mankind had come in its progress. An archduke may have had his hundred players in the palace, but he was surely not able to enjoy the same effect while travelling in his coach. Nowadays cars have their own superb hi-fi systems, and millions of homes have video machines with a choice of films which make the theatre antiquated beyond belief. All have access to such libraries that only archdukes possessed. We can cross the Atlantic in a few hours for a hundred pounds, and yet does all this indicate that we have reached the Promised Land? With three million out of work, it seemed as if everything that everyone once wanted has slipped out of our grasp. People can see revolution and mayhem on the telly every night while they eat their baked beans and fishfingers, and don't know what it is that keeps making them belch.

'I recognize that, sir.'

'What?'

'The music. It's *Israel in Egypt*. I more than recognize it. Pity we're not staying together. "Thou hast guided them in Thy strength." Lovely! I could sing every note, at one time.'

'How's that?'

He laughed. 'I used to be in the choral society.' He named a Lancashire town. 'Before we disbanded. I love Handel.'

'Who wouldn't?'

'You'd be surprised. But they were good days. They

didn't last long. Everybody listened to us, though. Even the local bigwigs! It don't happen anymore.'

'Why, I wonder?'

He was intent on the scenery, but said: 'Because we're in a wilderness. We don't fight. We've got everything to fight for, but we don't believe in God, so we can't. We're waiting for the days when "the extortion is at an end", and "the spoiling ceaseth". Isaiah, that. The whole earth is full of God's glory, and what have we done with it?'

He drove in silence, too embarrassed to talk while the man was so disheartened, angry that there was no answer. The television set lives for us, now that we have sold our birthright to the computers. He felt a tap on his shoulder. 'You can put me off here, sir.'

In case he ran out of petrol and had no money on him, he kept a five-pound note in the glove box. Sweating at the pain in his ribs, he reached across, and pressed the money into the man's hand. 'It'll buy you a meal on the way down to the smoke.'

He reminded Paul of that photograph of the Russian intellectual during the siege of Leningrad looking at a small piece of bread just issued to him, and wondering how he was going to go on living when it had gone. He parked on a bend, traffic whipping up behind. There was danger, and he wanted to move off quickly.

The man passed the note back. 'You're a champion, sir, thank you, but I've got some money. I sold my bike yesterday for thirty quid to tide me over. I'll be all right for a week or two.' He closed the door, and spoke through the open window. 'The music was lovely, though. A rare treat.'

Paul did not like himself. His gesture was cheap at the price. He'd had no option but to offer something because, as he had heard say: 'It's the good deeds you

208

don't do that God never forgives you for.'

The man refused his money again, and closed the door, crossing the road in front before Paul could take off. Holding the clipboard like a bus inspector he stationed himself by a crossroads. Another car drew up. When Paul looked at his map it was obvious that the direction the man took would set him back towards Warwick and Birmingham, not London. And in any case, would he go from Liverpool to London without a scrap of luggage? Even Whittington had his handkerchief on the end of a staff. Also, he wouldn't come this far east, but would keep to the M6 motorway and join the M1 south-east of Birmingham. What's more, his accent had nothing of Liverpool in it. He could have come from anywhere with such a neutral twang. Maybe he had changed his mind at the last minute, and decided to go somewhere else. He could be a plain-clothes policeman. They did such work, for reasons best known to themselves.

He regretted not having asked more questions. The untold story, or stories, nagged at him. He wanted to know about the man's parents, his wife and children, and a thousand facts without which he could not begin to imagine what he was really like. If he was a policeman what cover story would he have spun? To be lumbered with two tales for the price of one was worth giving anybody a lift.

But if the man was genuinely unemployed, and Paul thought he was, the possibility of their becoming familiar was overshadowed by the salient feature of work. Everything descended to the lowest common denominator of a person's occupation. Nothing else mattered. If he had work, he was one of the elect. If he had no work, he was one of the damned – not even in Limbo. Paul thought that if he had no work he would

happily give up his life to reading and study. He was
born that way. Curiosity would prevent him from being
idle or bored. But he spoke from supposition, not
experience. The poor were also those who could not
profitably fill a workless existence. For them there was
only television. How short had been that Golden Age
between work being a life of the jungle, and becoming a
luxury that those without it could not afford. Work was
either a fight for subsistence, conducive only to misery
and ill-health, or it was a state seen as nothing but
mindless bliss by those who had never had to lift a
finger. How many votes had Labour lost in the election
because they had promised to get everybody back to
work?

He switched again to *Israel in Egypt*.

X

He remembered Crawby youth hostel as having a
thatched roof and being situated on the edge of the
village. The present hostel had a covering of tin, and
was hidden in the shadow of the church.

A handsome magpie preened itself on the lawn. Two
Danish backpackers smoked their pipes at a circular
table, and Paul couldn't tell whether one of them, with
such androgynous features and a ponytail of hair, was
man or woman. A ginger cat systematically cleaned
itself. The place didn't open till half past five so he
searched for the former site of the hostel, nearer the
main road and closer to the pub. A grey warplane with
swept-back wings followed the fold of land to the south-
east.

He walked to the 'office' along a beamed corridor
and over reddish, well-worn tiles, booked in on his

pristine membership ticket, and rented a sheet-sleeping bag. Unlike the peppery gent of former times, the warden was a young woman, and her male assistant recognized Paul's name because of his television plays.

Upstairs he took the room farthest in, and opted for one of the lower bunks. The Danes, both male as it turned out, had the next room. He got his mess can from the car and emptied a tin of stew into it. With bread, and two oranges, he made a supper in the large kitchen equipped with pots, pans and cutlery. The Danes had already eaten, and no other wayfarers came that night.

To be alone was strange, at his age, and after the kind of life he had led. To sever connection with the known, on the off-chance of remembering a week from thirty-eight years ago, was unsettling. Nothing could justify the exercise unless there was something to be learned, an advantage to be gained, and so far nothing occurred to him. He felt foolish, and self-indulgent. At other moments he was more himself than he had been for years.

He went to the pub and sat through the long, slow demolition of a pint, then walked sleepily back while day was lapsing to read a few more chapters of Second Samuel in the hostel common room, the only place where one was allowed to smoke. Rules made him feel infantile – however sensible they were – not young. Not that he had grown used to freedom since being released from them. Other rules which one accepted voluntarily offered a different kind of protection, and built even stronger walls.

There were no motor noises this far from the main road, only the sound of birds and the soulless bark of a dog. The occasional hoot of an owl was more comical than melancholy. Lights were to be out at 10.30, and sleep came easily.

In the empty kitchen he made breakfast of tea, and bread and cheese, not knowing whether he would have felt more human if the place had been crowded with campers and excursionists. Either way, the sense of isolation would have prevailed, although the relief of people who had reached shelter after pedalling or hiking across the countryside had a quality which could not be forgotten. But it was midweek, and not the Bank Holiday as before.

Obliged to do something towards keeping the place clean before the membership card could be given back, he offered to tidy the kitchen. Muriel Fletcher would laugh, he thought, if she could see me wielding a sweeping brush. It'll make a funny yarn when I tell her, though in her newly-married state she won't – for a while anyway – be easy to reach. He couldn't remember what task he had done in 1945, but had a vague memory of picking cigarette ends from the dew-wet lawn with Sheffield and his mates.

Beyond Northampton a transport café had turned into La Bonne Auberge. Rockingham Forest was unaltered, but at Blatherdene there was no cottage serving tea for a shilling, or any other kind of tea. Perhaps the doubled-up old woman crossing the road, whom he missed by a foot or two, was the one who had made love to him. These days he wanted them young, and no such woman in any case would choose him, because they would see too clearly what kind of a person he was. All he remembered of the woman was her wonderful Tartar eyes. Where had they come from? He also thought he recalled the smell of her laundered knickers. But the eyes have it, and always would, the only place the broken spirit shows.

When he went into the post office shop at Kings Cliffe to buy cigars the woman said that the youth hostel had been the same building as the old Red Lion. The pub had also long since closed. He couldn't remember. Sandstone villages seemed all the same. The mind was a living dustbin that threw up impressions only to tantalize. To make such connection with the past was hardly worth the trouble. A foolproof technique for accurate recollection would in any case kill the memory with overwork. 'Oh why did I wake? When shall I sleep again?' he might have asked, when he got back into his car, the only habitation where he felt at home.

XI

The Palladian house of Burley lay on a hill. The view from the top would show the large new stretch of the reservoir, but he did not drive up to see it. He stayed by the main road in the knowledge that all good things are best enjoyed from a distance.

He leaned on a gate and let his binoculars enlarge the house ten times, wishing to envisage unity, and consider the fragments at leisure. To see the whole with sharp clarity, from as far away as possible, implied that there was a clear point to aim for. Only the naked eye could describe its parts.

The field glasses were the best that could be bought, and he never travelled without them. There were many objects he impulsively put into his car on setting out, as if the Bomb might go off during his journey and he would need such equipment to survive at least for a little while. It was comforting and practical. A shotgun and twenty rounds were concealed beneath the cardboard boxes.

The same force that had sent him on his travels from the age of eighteen would never allow him to kill himself. He sounded too certain to know it for sure. The man on the tank-bike near Kings Cliffe had shouted that the English were a nation of slaves, but Paul didn't think anyone existed in the world who was not. If all were equal in the sight of God, they were the slaves of God, because Death was his taskmaster. To thwart him in his work by suicide was to destroy creation with as much finality as those who might one day be responsible for beginning a nuclear war.

Binoculars showed the solid mansion in permanent occupation of the land it stood on, as if the owners had title to all the terrain which could be seen from the topmost rooms. He had no part of the house, and none of the land, yet felt that some item of it belonged to him, though he had no wish to own such a place. The world is divided between those who have their feet solidly in life, as if they're going to live forever, and those who, thumbing a lift from one day to the next, and from one year to another, belong nowhere because early on they set out with the idea of reaching a Utopian destination which could not exist anywhere except in the mind. But a desire for justice, freedom and equality for all had ended as a vague mixture of social comfort and self-realization for himself. Such a truth made him happy only insofar as it contained a warning that life without the pursuit of an ideal was an idle waste.

He didn't want to possess that large house circled in his field glasses, with its hundreds of acres and no doubt vast library, because at the end of his life he would find it painful to leave so much that he owned. Twenty years ago, thinking less of death, he might have wanted it, but nowadays he had more than sufficient space in which to live. His feeling had nothing to do with possession. He was interested in the house as a construction of plain and ornate bricks put together by an infant.

Even when he saw the house at seventeen his mind had gone back to babytime days on Crying Island, remembering how the schoolteacher, having read the Hebrew Bible to them till she was tired, made them sit in a circle not quite complete. Without daring to turn round, he heard the opening of a large cupboard. None of them had seen such a big one before coming to school. The rest of the world and all their future lives might have come out of that cupboard. Through the gap of the circle she bore a canvas bag and spilled its contents onto the floor.

The bricks, of many shapes and sizes, were for them to build with. Rain dimmed the tall windows. There was a short silence, in which planning was a moment in advance of action. Eyes and fingers laid the ground, made the height, fixed the bays, set the wings and blocked out windows. No light was bright enough. He arranged quadrants, balustrades and pediments with adventurous precision.

Conflict guided them, because war was always possible from a neighbour out of malice or envy, or due to some feeling impossible to give a name to. Lightning struck in the shape of a hand that knocked everything into ruins. Speed was important to complete a project of the heart, and give a glimpse of a paradise you had made yourself.

You learned early that nothing could last. If you leave the home area all you have left is memory. If you never depart from it the advance to death is short. All feints were diverted or attacks crushed. You sooner or later crumbled the house so that the bricks of endeavour could be scooped up into the bag and put back into that great cupboard from where all things came. Nothing was permanent, but building continued in your mind when it was no longer possible on the classroom floor. A lid was placed over the consciousness, and that which was enclosed became an inertial guiding force.

Ringed in his binoculars, the building on the hill might remain for a further three hundred years. While Edith Weston wept by Rutland Water no hint of megadoom cracked the green sweep from which the graceful mansion rose. The architect who had also played on the nursery floor with bricks and pieces may have forgotten such a pastime by the hour of his first commission. The realized vision was superimposed on the dream of infancy with playtime bricks. Geological layers of the spirit, not under anyone's control, assumed their power. The course was steered according to a lodestone buried in the earth.

When he got back from his first long bicycle ride, the aim of his life was fixed, though he did not know it. He did four years' service with some enjoyment, and broke the mould. He left England for the first time. He drank orange juice for the first time. He ate chicken for the first time. He wore underwear for the first time. He smoked cigars, stayed awake all night, learned a trade, and had a servant to make his bed and clean his boots. He served the King to the best of his ability and without embarrassment.

The road towards Oakham ran alongside a stream, his car compass indicating north-north-west as he combed through the last day of the cycle ride. Handel's oratorio played. Had he set out for the Promised Land, or been drowned in the Red Sea before he could get properly on his way? The magnificent chorus buoyed him up. Life was worth living, such music joining the two people of then and now.

One might travel like a king with his own chorus and

orchestra, but there was a barrier between Paul and the landscape. He felt no wind or thunderflies as on a bicycle, no headaching sun or pain in the legs, no breathlessness. He floated as if in a dream, without effort, entranced by the moving pictures of fields, woods and villages. Dogs could run out of cottage gates and chase him at their peril. He had been more of a king in former days, but things were much the same.

He passed a pub called the Noell Arms, and went by Victoria Hall. Did she know Edith Weston? He was going too fast to make up a story. He noticed the Crown Hotel, the Wheatsheaf, and the Black Horse where he had talked to the old man long since dead. Everybody's turn came, that was certain, even the swaddies who had argued with the consumptive woman in the fish and chip queue, no matter how far they walked or cycled or drove in their lives.

He stopped at the summit of Broughton Hill. Traffic of all types except bicycles passed in both directions. He edged the car as far as possible into the side and put on the hazard lights. A stack of cumulus lay above the haze, sunbeams like knives as if about to carve the delectable landscape and share it with all-powerful beings from another planet.

There was a warm breeze, so he left his jacket in the car, and looked at the view, listening to the last chorus of *Israel in Egypt*. There was no point using binoculars, because little detail of the landscape was clear. The Trent and the city were fifteen miles away, and only in clarity after rain were they visible. The Roman vein of the Fosse Way maintained its diagonal route across the county. He hoped that the Ukrainian man had married his farming woman and found happiness at last.

When he had last looked into the future from this point, expectations had been vague, but all the stronger for that. Not knowing what lay behind the impulse had made its power irresistible. He had ridden down into the adventurous murk. Since that time he had never been as long as six days out of contact with anyone. Two days of freedom, three at the most, but never as many as six. The mysteries of the past were more profound than those of the future. That 250-mile bicycle ride seemed dead only because it had done its work. To imagine that the deadness was in him was only a covering to hide the seed that still lived.

He did not complete the circle and go on, as he had before, down from the hill. A little gap was left undone. In that direction was a fecund ruin with which he wanted no apparent connection. In spite of danger from passing traffic he backed the car till he came to a lane to make a three-point turn. He drove towards London as fast as he could go, in a silence interrupted only when the piece of slate from the rooftop of Wishdale Abbey clattered to the side of the road.

Jerusalem, London, Wittersham 1983-4

The world's greatest novelists now available in Panther Books

J B Priestley

Angel Pavement	£2.50	☐
Saturn Over the Water	£1.95	☐
Lost Empires	£2.50	☐
It's An Old Country	£1.95	☐
The Shapes of Sleep	£1.75	☐
The Good Companions	£2.50	☐

Kingsley Amis

I Like It Here	£1.50	☐
That Uncertain Feeling	50p	☐
The Alteration	95p	☐
The Riverside Villas Murder	95p	☐

Alan Sillitoe

The Second Chance	£1.50	☐
Her Victory	£2.50	☐
The Lost Flying Boat	£1.95	☐

Dirk Bogarde

A Gentle Occupation	£2.50	☐
Voices in the Garden	£1.95	☐

To order direct from the publisher just tick the titles you want and fill in the order form.

The world's greatest novelists now available in Panther Books

To order direct from the publisher just tick the titles you want and fill in the order form.

The world's greatest novelists now available in Panther Books

Kurt Vonnegut

Breakfast of Champions	£1.95	☐
Mother Night	£1.95	☐
Slaughterhouse 5	£1.95	☐
Player Piano	£1.95	☐
Welcome to the Monkey House	£1.95	☐
God Bless You, Mr Rosewater	£1.95	☐
Happy Birthday, Wanda June	£1.95	☐
Slapstick	£1.95	☐
Wampeters Foma & Granfalloons (non-fiction)	£2.50	☐
Between Time and Timbuktu (illustrated)	£1.50	☐
Jailbird	£1.95	☐
Palm Sunday	£1.95	☐
Deadeye Dick	£1.95	☐

John Barth

The Sot-Weed Factor	£3.95	☐
Giles Goat-Boy	£2.95	☐
The End of the Road	£1.50	☐
The Floating Opera	£1.95	☐
Letters	£3.95	☐
Chimera	£1.95	☐
Sabbatical	£2.50	☐

Tim O'Brien

Going After Cacciato	£1.25	☐
If I Die in a Combat Zone	£1.25	☐

To order direct from the publisher just tick the titles you want
and fill in the order form. **GF481**

The world's greatest novelists now available in Panther Books

Simon Raven
***'Alms for Oblivion'* series**

Fielding Gray	£1.95	☐
Sound the Retreat	£1.95	☐
The Sabre Squadron	£1.95	☐
The Rich Pay Late	£1.95	☐
Friends in Low Places	£1.95	☐
The Judas Boy	£1.95	☐
Places Where They Sing	£1.95	☐
Come Like Shadows	£2.50	☐
Bring Forth the Body	£1.95	☐
The Survivors	£1.95	☐

Other Titles

The Roses of Picardie	£1.50	☐
The Feathers of Death	35p	☐
Doctors Wear Scarlet	30p	☐

Paul Scott
The Raj Quartet

The Jewel in the Crown	£2.95	☐
The Day of the Scorpion	£2.95	☐
The Towers of Silence	£2.95	☐
A Division of the Spoils	£2.95	☐

Other Titles

The Bender	£1.95	☐
The Corrida at San Feliu	£2.50	☐
A Male Child	£1.50	☐
The Alien Sky	£2.50	☐
The Chinese Love Pavilion	£2.50	☐
The Mark of the Warrior	£1.95	☐
Johnnie Sahib	£2.50	☐
The Birds of Paradise	£1.50	☐
Staying On	£1.95	☐

To order direct from the publisher just tick the titles you want
and fill in the order form.

GF381

The world's greatest novelists now available in Panther Books

John Barth

The Sot-Weed Factor	£3.95	☐
Giles Goat-Boy	£2.95	☐
The End of the Road	£1.50	☐
The Floating Opera	£1.95	☐
Letters	£3.95	☐
Chimera	£1.95	☐
Sabbatical	£2.50	☐

John Banville

Kepler	£1.95	☐
Dr Copernicus	£2.50	☐
Birchwood	£1.95	☐
The Newton Letter	£1.95	☐

Christopher Hope

A Separate Development	£1.95	☐
Private Parts	£1.95	☐

To order direct from the publisher just tick the titles you want and fill in the order form.

GF881

All these books are available at your local bookshop or newsagent, or can be ordered direct from the publisher.,

To order direct from the publisher just tick the titles you want and fill in the form below.

Name_____

Address _____

_____

Send to:
Panther Cash Sales
PO Box 11, Falmouth, Cornwall TR10 9EN.

Please enclose remittance to the value of the cover price plus:

UK 45p for the first book, 20p for the second book plus 14p per copy for each additional book ordered to a maximum charge of £1.63.

BFPO and Eire 45p for the first book, 20p for the second book plus 14p per copy for the next 7 books, thereafter 8p per book.

Overseas 75p for the first book and 21p for each additional book.